A Deadly Delivery

APRIL FERNSBY

DEDICATION

For Rosie and Eve

Chapter 1

"Are you going in or are you going to stand there like a stuffed lemon?"

"Pardon?" I focused on the red-faced man who had just shouted at me.

He gave me an irritated look, jabbed his thumb at the café door and snapped, "In or out? If you're not going in, then shift out of my way. I'm already running late this morning, and I don't need any further delays. Well? In or out?"

"Out." I removed my hand from the café door and stood to one side to let the impatient man enter Erin's Café.

He treated me to another annoyed look before pushing the door open and stepping through.

As the door slowly closed behind him, I caught a glimpse of a young woman inside. Erin, my sister. She was fifteen years younger than me and had been a surprise addition to our family. Mum had been the most surprised.

There she was; standing behind the counter of her café and giving that rude man the most patient of looks as she smiled at him. I hadn't seen her in two years. Two full years without seeing my little sister. We'd spoken on the phone a few times, but those had been stilted conversations.

Well, I couldn't face her, not after what I'd done to her. I was a fool to come here and think I could apologise. I couldn't expect her to forgive me. I couldn't even forgive myself.

I drank in the sight of her beautiful, elfin-like face as the door finally closed. My heart missed a beat as she looked my way at the last second before the door shut in my face. She looked tired, really tired. There was something else too. In that fraction of a second, I could sense it.

I pushed the door open and rushed into the café. Erin noticed me and her hand shook as she handed over a cardboard cup to the rude man. I was aware of him moaning about something or other, but I didn't pay him any further attention. Now that I was closer to Erin, I could see the small lines around her eyes. Her skin was pale and the pale-purple circles under her eyes indicated she hadn't had a good night's sleep for a long time.

I gave her a small smile. I hoped she wouldn't shout at me and demand that I leave. I wouldn't blame her if she did.

The rude man snatched the cup from Erin and said loudly, "This better not be cold. It was distinctly on the tepid side yesterday. I had to stick it in the microwave when I got to work. I should charge you for the electricity I used."

Erin took her attention off me and said to the man, "I'm very sorry about that. That coffee is piping hot."

"It had better be," the man warned.

His rudeness was annoying me now. I turned my head and glowered at him. Couldn't he see there was something going on here? Couldn't he sense the atmosphere between Erin and me? Didn't he realise he was in the way and should clear off?

The man jumped as he caught my hard look. He pulled his cup towards him in a protective manner, turned around and scuttled out of the café without another word.

Erin burst into laughter and said, "I'd forgotten your angry look! What was it Mum used to say? You'd scare the butter right off the toast with that angry look of yours."

I relaxed my features and smiled at Erin. "I don't have an angry look."

"Yeah, you do. It's like this." She scrunched her face up and attempted to glower at me. Her face was too beautiful to look angry. And the happy twinkle in her eyes only made her look cuter.

A huge wave of love washed over me and tears sprang to my eyes. I blurted out, "I'm sorry! So very sorry. I'm an idiot. An out and out idiot. I have no excuses. I don't expect you to forgive me. I just wanted to say I'm sorry."

Erin swiftly came out from behind the counter and moved over to me. She pulled me into a tight hug and said, "There's nothing to be sorry about. I've told you that over and over again. But, yes, you are an idiot. I knew that from the second I saw you. Even though I was a newborn, I knew you were an idiot. A nitwit. A ninny. A pudding-head."

I could hear the laughter in her voice. I stayed in her embrace and said, "You smell of cake."

She laughed and released me. "I always smell of cake. I made a Victoria sponge this morning. Take a seat at the counter and I'll cut you a generous slice. How about a cup of tea? Or would you prefer a coffee?" The twinkle in her eyes intensified. "It might be on the tepid side, but that's the chance you've got to take in my café."

She put her hand on my arm and took me closer to the counter. She pulled a stool out and pushed me gently onto it. As she moved back behind the counter, I had a quick look around the café. I was surprised to see only a few tables were occupied. This used to be the busiest time of the day. Something was definitely wrong here.

Erin placed a steaming cup of tea in front of me along with a huge slice of cake. She leant her elbows on the counter and studied me.

"What?" I said. "Why are you looking at me like that?"

"Because I love you. And it's wonderful to see you again. I can't believe it's been so long. We've got a lot to catch up on." She frowned. "You look lighter. You look different. That worry in your eyes has gone. What's happened to you?"

I felt my mouth twitching and was worried I was going to break into a full grin. Trying to keep serious, I said, "It's over."

A glimmer of hope came into Erin's eyes. "Over? Do you mean…?"

I gave her a nod. "Yes, my marriage is over. Or it will be soon."

Erin raised her hands in the air and pumped them with joy. She let out a holler of delight and then twirled around on the spot. One of her customers let out a quiet tut.

Erin grabbed my hands. "Tell me that again. Slowly. I want all the details. Who left who? Was it you? It must have been. When did you finally come to your senses? Oh! I don't care! I'm just glad you did."

I grinned at her. "It was a few weeks ago. You're right about me coming to my senses. It hit me one day when I was cleaning his shirts. I stood there and looked at the lipstick on his collar. Yes, I know. What a cliché. Lipstick on his collar. And there was perfume on his shirt too. I stared at his dirty washing and thought what a fool I was. To ignore his cheating for years was one thing, but to do his washing after he'd been with his girlfriend was a step too far." My grin died and I swallowed. "Erin, how could I allow him to treat me like that?"

She squeezed my hands. "That's a mystery to us all. You deserve a medal for staying married to Gavin Booth for so long." She looked over my shoulder as someone came into the café. "We are going to have a long and detailed talk about this soon. I want to know everything. I'm here for you. I won't allow you to go through a painful divorce on your own."

My chin wobbled. "Thank you. I didn't just come here to tell you about Gavin, I wanted to apologise for what I did. And I want to know how you are and what's been going on with you. Erin, you look tired. Are you well?"

Erin released my hands and gave me a bright smile. "I'm in tip-top health. My bread delivery is here. Let me sort this out and we'll talk again in a minute or two. Eat your cake!"

Erin smiled at someone behind me. I turned around in my seat and observed the young woman who was walking towards us carrying a stack of baskets filled with bread.

A dizzy feeling attacked me and I grabbed the counter for support. It was happening again.

Chapter 2

Ever since I could remember, I'd had psychic abilities. It was a blessing or a curse depending on what I experienced. It was a blessing when I saw something wonderful in a friend's future, especially when they were going through a difficult time. It was a curse when I saw a close relative reaching the end of their days like I experienced with my wonderful grandma. I didn't just get the visions of what could happen in the future; sometimes I got the smells and tastes to go with them. As if that wasn't confusing enough, I sometimes got images of the past.

With one thing and another over the years, I'd ignored my psychic abilities, and my visions had slowed down. I hadn't had one for a while.

But I was having one now. I had no doubts about that.

I looked closer at the young woman who was carrying the bread baskets. There were two shadows behind her. One belonged to her, but the other one didn't belong to anyone. The second shadow followed her across the café floor with its hands held out. It was hard to say if it was male or female. The shadow suddenly thrust its hands towards the young woman's shadow and pushed her on the back. The woman's shadow tumbled forward and I saw her mouth open in a scream.

I felt someone tapping my shoulder. I looked that way and saw Erin giving me a confused look. She said, "Karis, are you alright? You've gone a funny colour."

A quick glance back at the floor showed me the spooky shadow had now vanished. I cleared my throat and said, "Yes! Course I am. Sorry. I just drifted off there for a moment."

Erin gave me a long look before saying, "Karis, this is Carmel. She works for Nithercott's Bread."

The young woman put the bread baskets on a nearby table and turned her friendly face towards me. She said, "Hi. Erin's mentioned you a few times, but we've never met. Would you like a free sample of bread? We've got some new sesame seed rolls that we've been working on. They're low in salt and we've even got the gluten-free variety." She reached into a basket and handed me a package of four rolls. She took a card from her jeans and gave me that too. "I'd love it if you could give some feedback on our website. If that's not too much trouble?"

I took the card and mumbled, "Thank you. I'll do that." I was finding it hard to meet Carmel's eyes. The vision of someone attacking her was playing over and over in my mind like a horror movie on repeat.

Carmel turned to Erin and continued, "How's the new bread recipe going down with your customers?"

Erin gave me another look before turning to Carmel. "They love it. I didn't tell them it was a new recipe until they'd tasted it. You know what people are like! Your classic loaf is loved by many, and if I'd have told my customers beforehand it had been changed, they would have made their minds up instantly that they wouldn't like it."

Carmel nodded. "Tell me about it. You'd think Mr Nithercott had made a deal with the devil instead of improving his classic loaf. You wouldn't believe the complaints we've had. Even death threats!"

"Really?" I said sharply. "What kind of death threats? Have you been attacked?" I was hoping the vision I'd seen was a remnant of the past.

Carmel gave me a puzzled look. "No, I haven't been attacked. It's Mr Nithercott who's received the death threats. The improved recipe is healthier, but some people don't care about that. They've taken it as a personal insult." She smiled at Erin. "I'm pleased your customers like it. Can I count on your continued orders?"

Erin's smile seemed slightly forced as she replied, "As long as I've got a café, then you're my supplier. Have you got time for a cuppa? Perhaps some cake?"

Carmel patted her stomach. "I'd better not. Mr Nithercott has got me sampling all the new products we're rolling out. I'll be needing some new jeans at this rate. Erin, I've got some new products in the basket. Could I be cheeky and ask you to sample them, please? I trust your judgement."

Erin looked towards the baskets. "I'd love to. What have you got in there?"

"The usual stuff, but with improvements." She waggled her eyebrows. "We've got some exotic products too. Don't be too scandalized, but we've got rolls with cinnamon in them."

Erin let out a mock cry of outrage. "Cinnamon! In bread! Carmel Johnson, this is Yorkshire, not New York! Whatever is going on in that bread factory? You've all gone mad."

Carmel laughed. "It's my fault. I keep coming up with these new things. You'll like the cinnamon ones. They're lovely with a strong coffee or a hot chocolate. We've even got small loaves with seeds in them and we've added protein to them too. It's what people want these days."

Erin shook her head. "Mad. That's what you are. Leave my café immediately before I call the bread police."

Carmel moved towards the baskets. "I'll take these through to the back and let myself out through the back door. Thanks again for your support, Erin. You don't know how much it means to me. I wish all my customers were like you." She picked the baskets up, flashed me a goodbye smile and went through to the kitchen area.

Once she'd gone, Erin gave me a sharp look. "What did you see?"

"Pardon?" I tried to look away.

Erin tapped me sharply on the shoulder. "You saw something when Carmel came in. I could see it on your face. You had one of your vision things, didn't you? Tell me what you saw."

I sighed. There was no point arguing with Erin. Unlike many people, she completely understood about my psychic abilities. I told her about the second shadow.

Erin frowned. "What does that mean? Did you pick up on anything else? Did you smell anything?"

I shook my head. "It could be nothing. I don't know whether it was from the future or the past. For all I know, a disgruntled customer could have shoved her a few weeks ago."

Erin's lips pressed together and she folded her arms. I could tell what she was thinking. She said, "Your visions are not to be taken lightly. They always mean something."

I said, "You're right. You should tell her what I saw. I don't care if she thinks I'm crazy. This could be a warning for her to watch out for angry customers."

Erin nodded and tilted her head towards the kitchen. "That's the back door closing. She must have left. I've got her number. I'll try her on that in a minute or two." She unfolded her arms and pointed to my untouched cake. "What's wrong with that? You haven't had one bite."

"I'm sorry. The vision thing made me lose my appetite." I looked at the clock on the wall behind Erin. "Oh heck! Is that the time? I'm meeting my solicitor in ten minutes to discuss the divorce settlement. I don't want to miss that."

"I don't want you to miss it either. The sooner you get officially divorced, the better. I'll keep this cake for you. You can collect it when you come over for dinner tonight." She held her hand up to ward off my objections. "We've got a lot of things to talk about. I will see you at eight o'clock."

I hesitated a second. "Will Robbie be there?"

She gave me a gentle smile. "He's my husband. Of course he'll be there. He'll be delighted to see you. And he'll be overjoyed about your divorce news."

"Even after…" I couldn't complete my sentence as fresh shame came over me.

Erin shook her head slowly. "Robbie loves you as much as I do. Come over tonight and we'll sort this confusion out. He doesn't blame you for any of it, and neither do I." She laughed. "In fact, he's been round to your house many times over these last two years to try and sort things out between us."

"Has he? I never saw him."

She gave me a pointed look. "That's because you never answered the door to him. Your fool of a husband did." She broke into a huge smile. "I must correct myself. Your ex-husband. Karis, hasn't that got a lovely ring to it? Gavin Booth is going to be your ex-husband. It's giving me a warm glow to think that."

I couldn't help but smile at her dreamy expression. I stood up and said, "You're weird."

"So are you." She flapped her hands at me. "Go. Meet that solicitor. Get divorced. I want all the juicy details later."

I rushed around to her and gave her a hug. "I'm so glad I came into your café. So very glad. I've missed you so much."

"Me too." She patted my back. "We'll have a good catch-up later."

I took my arms away and said, "You will phone Carmel, won't you? As soon as possible?"

Erin produced her phone from her pocket. "I'll do it right now."

I said goodbye and left the café feeling a million times better than when I entered. Well, perhaps not that much. Erin looked tired and her café was almost empty. That wasn't right. I'd get the truth from her later about what was going on there. And the business about Carmel's possible attack was niggling at my mind. Hopefully, Erin would get through to Carmel in time to prevent anything terrible happening.

I nodded to myself. Yes, that's what would happen. Carmel would be alright. I needed to clear my head of all thoughts for now. I needed to be level-headed when I met my solicitor. Gavin Booth was going to be my ex-husband. A smile alighted on my lips. Yes, it did have a good ring to it.

Chapter 3

Later that night, Robbie welcomed me with open arms into the home he shared with Erin. He'd opened the front door as I'd parked in the driveway, and as soon as I was close enough, he had wrapped his big arms around me and gave me the longest hug. It was like being embraced by a friendly bear. Robbie was one of my favourite people in the whole world. There was something so capable and confident about him. He knew a lot of information about a lot of things. He would lend a hand to anyone at any time. If you had a problem, Robbie was your man.

Problems with your washing machine? Robbie would fix it in no time.

Issues with your car? Leave it to Robbie.

Concerns over your roof? Robbie would have his ladder out and be on the roof in a minute.

An apocalypse? Yep. I'm sure Robbie would be able to deal with that too in his no-nonsense and sensible way.

Robbie was a good man. Which is why I felt so incredibly guilty about what I'd done to him.

When he finally let me go, he looked down at me with his kind eyes and said, "It's so good to have you here, Karis. I can't tell you how happy I am to see you again. I'm over the moon to see you've made up with Erin. Not that there was anything to make up. No, it's all been a misunderstanding." He wagged a finger at me in a jovial manner. "And that's what we're going to get sorted out right now. Come in! Come in! We're having pre-dinner drinks tonight in the living room. We've gone all fancy and posh. We don't do this for just anyone, you know."

He took my coat and handbag and hung them on the end of the bannister. As he walked down the hallway, I winced when I noticed how pronounced his limp was. Fresh guilt settled in my stomach and killed my appetite. I wouldn't be able to eat a thing tonight.

Robbie led me into the living room where Erin was waiting with a glass of wine for me. She was wearing make-up and looked more awake than she had earlier in the café.

She handed me the wine and said, "It's non-alcoholic before you start going on about driving. I'm having the same."

I took the glass. "Non-alcoholic? You? Why?"

She shrugged. "It wouldn't be fair on you if I got drunk. I'm being thoughtful and kind. Make the most of it. Sit down. Let's get this elephant out of the room before we have anything to eat."

Robbie let out a loud guffaw and patted his round stomach. "Are you calling me an elephant? I know I've put on a few pounds, but that's no way to talk about your loving husband." He took my elbow and led me over to the sofa. "Sit next to me, Karis, and let me have a good look at you."

I sat down and Robbie turned his attention to me.

Erin sat in the armchair opposite us and said, "It's like I told you earlier, Robbie, she looks lighter, doesn't she? Like a huge, useless weight has been lifted from her shoulders." She gave a sniff of disapproval. "That's exactly what has happened. A useless weight called Gavin Booth has been lifted from her shoulders. Karis, you are still going ahead with the divorce, aren't you? Course you are. You look happy. You can tell me what the solicitor said later. Let's get this other issue out of the way first. Robbie, it's over to you."

I put my glass down on the table in front of me and declared, "Let me talk. I have to say sorry. No, sorry isn't good enough. I regret what happened every day."

Robbie held a hand up to hush me. He said, "No, listen to me, Karis, it wasn't your fault. Let's clear this up once and for all."

I shook my head vehemently. "I'm the one who had the vision. I'm the one who saw you going into that post office. I saw the date on the wall. I saw the face of the man who shot you. I knew enough to warn you!" My voice rose with each sentence.

Robbie said, "There are always risks with my job. I knew that when I joined the police force. You had nothing to do with that man who shot me. No one could have stopped him." He gave me a smile and rested his hand on his leg. "He only clipped my leg. It could have been worse."

"But I saw it before it happened! I could have stopped it." I clasped my hands together in agitation. "You can't patrol the streets anymore. You loved doing that. You're stuck behind a desk now. It's all my fault."

Erin cried out, "Enough! Karis, you did what you could. Have you forgotten how poorly you were when you had that vision? You'd just had your hysterectomy. You couldn't get out of bed. You told Gavin about your vision. He promised he'd tell Robbie, but the lying piece of scum didn't tell him."

I lowered my head and said quietly, "When I found out about the shooting, Gavin said he didn't tell Robbie about my vision because he was too embarrassed to do so. He said I was probably having hallucinations because of the painkillers I was taking." I lifted my head. "I should have phoned you to make sure Gavin had warned you, but Gavin had taken my phone away because he didn't want anyone to disturb me. And I let him. But I should have insisted. I should have done more."

Robbie placed his bear-like hand over my clasped ones and said, "You did all that you could. Gavin made his decision based on what he thought was right. I was shot. I wasn't killed. I've got a limp which gives me an air of mystery. And I now have a desk job which means I don't have to go out in the cold. The worse thing that came out of this was you losing touch with us."

"I couldn't face you," I replied. "I felt so bad and wished I'd tried harder to let you know what was going to happen."

I recalled Gavin's face when we found out what had happened to Robbie. He'd merely shrugged and said that was the risk you took when you were a copper. He didn't feel the slightest shred of guilt over not telling Robbie about my vision. I didn't tell Erin and Robbie any of this now.

Erin said softly, "We never blamed you for Robbie's injuries. Never. We don't want you to blame yourself either. Can we put it in the past now? Forever?"

I looked at her kind face and said, "I would love that."

She grinned at me. "Good. That's settled. Tell me about your meeting with the solicitor. How much are you going to get in the settlement? Has Gavin got millions stashed away somewhere? I bet he has. You hear what dodgy things financial brokers get up to all the time. I'm surprised he never ended up in prison. I bet—"

"Erin," Robbie interrupted her. "I'm sure Gavin doesn't partake in illegal business dealings."

"Erm. He sort of does," I began. "He'd put many investments in my name over the years. At the time, he told me it was because of tax issues and that he'd transfer them over to his name when the time was right. It seems he forgot to do that and I now have lucrative stocks and shares in my name."

"How lucrative?" Erin leaned forwards.

I smiled at her. "Quite a lot. It's going to annoy Gavin. He's going to be furious when he finds out."

Erin nodded. "Good. Great. I hope he cries."

"Erin," Robbie gave her a warning look.

"Don't you look at me like that, Robbie Terris. You're a policeman. You know what these financial types get up to. Well, some of them. That's probably why Gavin didn't come round here often. He couldn't face you and those probing eyes of yours. You're like a human lie detector. One look into those lovely eyes, and the truth comes spilling out." She smiled at him. "Or is that just the effect you have on me?"

Robbie chuckled. "It's the amazing power I have on you, my love. Can we have something to eat now? We don't normally eat this late. My stomach is confused." He looked at me. "Are you ready to eat? Please say yes."

I nodded. "I am. I'm glad we cleared the air." I still felt guilty, but I would deal with that in my own time. "Erin, did you get in touch with Carmel?"

"I did. I told her it was me who'd experienced the vision. As expected, she laughed. But she did say she'd take good care of herself and keep away from anyone who looked like they'd cause her harm." Erin stood up. "Come on, Karis, there's nothing else you can do about Carmel. She's going to be fine."

Chapter 4

"Carmel Johnson is dead."

"What? Erin, say that again." I lowered the sheet of paper I was looking at and gripped my phone tightly.

Erin's voice broke as she repeated the words, "Carmel Johnson is dead. I've just found out."

I put the legal papers to one side and stood up. "Are you at the café now? Are you on your own?"

I heard a couple of sniffs before Erin replied, "Yes, I'm on my own at the café. Karis, you were right to be worried about Carmel. She fell down some stairs at the bread factory. It happened yesterday." She stopped speaking and I could hear her sobs.

"Don't say another word," I told her. "I'm at home but I'm coming over right now."

"Thank you," Erin said quietly.

I made it to the café in fifteen minutes. As soon as I entered, I dashed over to Erin and put my arms around her. She looked as pale as a bleached sheet and she was shaking.

She said, "It's such a shock. I'd only known her for a few months, but she was such a lovely woman. I never got the chance to tell her how much I loved those cinnamon rolls she left for me yesterday." She began to cry.

I stroked her back and took the opportunity to look around the café. It was empty. It should have been full of customers wanting a hot, cooked breakfast.

I said to Erin, "I'm going to close the café. You should go home."

Erin moved away from me. "I can't close the café! I never close the café. Not at this time of the day."

I waved my hand at the empty tables. "There's no one here. You can close it for a short while. At least long enough for me to make you a cup of tea."

"I suppose ten minutes won't hurt," Erin relented. She moved over to the door and locked it. She turned the sign to Closed.

By the time she came back to the counter, I'd poured her a cup of tea. I made one for myself too. I took Erin over to the nearest table and sat her down. I was going to put the cup in her hands, but they were trembling too much at the moment. I placed our cups on the table and moved my chair closer to Erin's.

I said gently, "Tell me what happened. How did you find out about Carmel?"

"Travis told me. He used to deliver my bread months ago before Carmel took over his round." Her mouth twisted slightly in disgust. "I've never liked Travis. He was never on time and he often gave me loaves which had been squashed. And he complained about everything. It was like the world was out to get him. I was glad when Carmel started to deliver my bread instead. I'm going to miss seeing her cheerful face." She looked down at the table.

"What did Travis tell you?"

She looked back at me. "He said there'd been an accident at the factory yesterday. It was late afternoon. Carmel had fallen down some stairs and broken her neck. It was Travis who'd found her. Karis, your vision was right. I should have been more forceful with Carmel when I spoke to her. I should have told her to avoid going anywhere dangerous. I should have told her to go home, get into bed and stay there."

I rested my hand on Erin's arm. "And what do you think Carmel would have said to that? I've tried to warn many people about the things I've seen in my visions. Most of them ignore me. Many mock me. Well, you know what I've been through. It's never easy trying to explain these things. You did what you could."

She shook her head. "It wasn't enough. Karis, I think Carmel must have been pushed down those stairs. She must have. It's too much of a coincidence."

"Did Travis give you any more information? Did he tell you where those stairs were or if anyone saw Carmel falling?"

She turned tear-filled eyes to me. "I was in shock when he told me. I couldn't think straight. He was complaining about something, but I've no idea what. I didn't even check the products he delivered. Karis, what are we going to do about this?"

I removed my hand from her arm and reached for my tea. "What can we do?"

"I don't know, but we have to do something. You saw Carmel being pushed. And now she's dead. It wasn't an accident. We've got to prove that."

"I can't walk into the police station and tell them about my vision. They'll lock me up." I sipped my tea and tried to avoid Erin's gaze.

She tapped her hand on the table. "Luckily for us, we know a handsome officer of the law who believes in your visions. He won't lock you up."

I put my cup down. "I don't know, Erin. I don't want to put Robbie in a difficult position. What will his colleagues think?"

The front door opened and Robbie walked in. He gave us a grim smile and said, "I thought you might have closed the café." He held up a key. "I always have my universal key with me. You never know when it might come in useful. I've just heard about Carmel Johnson."

Erin let out a fresh sob.

Robbie jogged over to her side and pulled a chair up next to her. He put his arm around her shoulders and looked at me. "Erin's already told me about your vision concerning Carmel. Tell me exactly what you saw."

I did so and imitated the actions of the second shadow.

Robbie nodded. "From your vision, it seems Carmel could have been pushed to her death. The initial reports show it to be an accident, but there are no witnesses apart from a chap called Travis. He's the one who found her."

Erin wiped her tears away. "She was pushed. Someone killed her. Robbie, you have to treat this as murder."

He brushed a lock of hair off her face. "I have every faith in Karis' visions just like you do, my love. I'm not dealing with this case, but I'll have a word with the investigating officer."

My heart sank. "They'll think I'm mad."

"Don't be so hard on the police force," Robbie said. "We rely a lot on our hunches and gut feelings. We're all psychic to some degree, though not many would admit it. You leave it with me, Karis. I'll give the investigating officer your details and tell him to speak to you."

Erin asked, "Do you know who'll be dealing with it?"

"I don't. It's a new chap who's come up from London. I haven't met him yet." He gave her a smile. "I'll phone him in a minute. I've taken the rest of the day off so that I can look after you."

"But the café?" Erin protested. "I can't leave it closed all day."

Robbie gave Erin a look which I couldn't decipher. Being psychic was all well and good when it worked, but there were times when I couldn't pick up on anything.

Robbie said softly, "A day away from the café won't matter, not in the general scheme of things. I'll have a quick tidy up and then we'll go home. Let me take care of you. That's what husbands do for their wives."

Erin leaned her head against Robbie's chest.

I felt a stab of jealousy. Gavin had never shown me such concern. Never. Now that I was getting a divorce from him, all his faults which I'd ignored were jumping out at me constantly. It was one bad memory after the other.

Erin said to me, "Karis, why don't you come home with us? I'll make us something to eat while we wait for Robbie's colleague to get in touch with you."

"As tempting as that is, I'd better get home. I need to go through some papers the solicitor gave me. I want to get this divorce finalised as soon as possible." I stood up and added, "I'll phone you later."

Robbie gave me a reassuring smile. "I'll take care of Erin. Phone us if there's anything you need."

I returned his smile before leaving the café. What I needed was a whole new set of memories concerning my soon-to-be ex-husband. The ones I had of him were too painful.

As I drove home, I forced my thoughts to focus on Carmel. It couldn't be a coincidence that she'd died after my vision. Had she been pushed to her death? It was too horrible to think about. But if she had been murdered, I knew I'd have to do all that I could to help the police. I'd let Robbie down when I could have taken action and I wasn't going to do that to Carmel.

Thoughts of Carmel fled my mind as I pulled into my driveway. Someone was trying to break into my house. I parked up, walked over to the would-be intruder and tapped them on the shoulder.

Chapter 5

Gavin jabbed his key at the lock and yelled at me, "Why won't my key work? What have you done to the door?"

I said calmly, "I've had the locks changed. Can you stop bashing your key against my new locks, please?"

Rage infused Gavin's face. "You've done what?"

"Changed the locks," I repeated.

Gavin thrust his useless key in my face. "You had no right to do that! This is my house and you can't keep me out!"

I pushed the key to one side. "Not according to my solicitor. This house is in my name."

"That's a mistake and you know it!" Gavin was almost snarling at me now. "Just like those investments I put in your name. It was a temporary situation. This house and those investments belong to me!"

I took a step back. "I'm not going to discuss legal matters with you. You should get your solicitor to talk to mine."

Gavin's angry expression changed. His new one was even worse. I'd seen him with that same look on his face when he was attempting to outwit a business rival. It was a sneaky, calculating look.

He lowered the key and gave me a wide smile. His tone was softer as he said, "Karis, why has it come to this? Can't we have a civil conversation without getting our solicitors involved? Let's go inside and you can make me a cup of coffee. We'll get this legal business sorted out in minutes. It's not as complicated as your solicitor is probably making out."

I didn't care for his condescending tone one bit. I stood my ground and replied, "You're not coming into my house. I won't be discussing any legal matters with you. Can you leave my property now?"

Panic flashed into Gavin's eyes and his smile wavered. "Let's not get silly about this. You know it's my money which paid for this house. It was my money behind those investments."

"Then why did you put them in my name?" I gave Gavin a defiant look. My solicitor had informed me of the reasons why Gavin might have done that. He also pointed out Gavin had made a grave mistake in doing so as the house and investments were legally mine and there was nothing Gavin could do about it.

Gavin's smile left his face altogether. "I don't know why you're being so stubborn about this. You know you haven't got a head for business. Let me inside and I'll try to explain the difficult parts for you. You'll soon see it's in your interests to transfer those assets to me."

"No, thanks. Are you leaving or do I have to call the police?"

Gavin sighed and ran a hand through his dyed hair. It was another calculating move which I'd seen him use before.

He gave me a sympathetic smile. "Karis, does it have to be like this? Can't we work things out? We have done before. I don't see what the problem is this time."

"I've overlooked your affairs for too long. I wasn't willing to do that anymore. I've finally found some self-respect. Gavin, I deserve better than you." I had never stood up to him like this before. It felt good.

He shook his head slowly. "Affairs? What are you talking about? I haven't had any affairs. It's just your overactive imagination. You know what you're like."

I gritted my teeth. My patience was trickling away like water down a drain. Keeping my voice controlled, I said, "I know all about your affairs. I know the names of the women involved. I know where you met them." I took a moment to steady my nerves. "And I know what you did with them."

Gavin snorted with derision. "You're mad. I always knew that and now you've confirmed it." He gave me a mocking smile. "Did you see me in those idiotic visions of yours?" He actually made quote marks in the air.

That was too much for me. All the anger I felt for him bubbled up. It was followed by intense feelings of shame at myself for putting up with him.

I said, "I know you don't believe in my visions, but let me try to convince you otherwise. Not only did I get images of who you were with, but I was also treated to certain smells and sounds. It turned my stomach."

Malice glinted in his eyes. He reached into his pocket and produced his phone. He tapped the screen and held it up. "Carry on. I've set my phone to record. Does your solicitor know about your visions? Mine does. She said she'd need proof if we're to use that against you."

"Against me? What do you mean?"

"I'm going to prove you're mentally unstable. My solicitor advised me not to, but she'll change her mind when I provide her with evidence. Carry on. Explain clearly what your visions are. This is going to be interesting."

I clenched my hands at my side. He was not going to treat me like some freak show. I began, "The first woman was Cindy. She wore cheap perfume and too much make-up. You met her in a hotel on the night I went into labour with Lorrie. Do you remember the night our daughter was born? You told me you were on a business meeting. You had a lot of those, didn't you? I saw you in the hotel room when Mum phoned you to let you know about Lorrie. You told Cindy to shush, but she giggled. Do you remember that?"

Gavin's voice was less certain now. "No, I don't remember that. You must have dreamt it."

I continued, "There was Brenda after Cindy. I liked her. She was always friendly when I turned up at your office. She must have felt guilty. She wore Chanel Number Five and she liked the seaside. You took her to Blackpool on weekends and stayed at that hotel where we'd had our honeymoon. I thought that was rather tacky, even for you. You even took Brenda to the same fish and chip place. She had mushy peas with hers. I could smell the vinegar on them."

Gavin lowered his phone a fraction. "You can't prove any of this."

"I don't want to prove anything. I want you to know that my visions are real. Let me go on."

I couldn't stop myself from telling Gavin about all the things I'd witnessed. Every single painful one. I wanted him to know the hurt and betrayal I'd felt with each one. Despite my best efforts, I hadn't been able to stop the visions coming. I'd never told anyone about them. I was too ashamed to.

By this point, Gavin had put his phone away and he looked ever so slightly embarrassed.

But I hadn't finished with him. I needed to get it all out. It was like an uncontrollable purge and I was feeling better by the second.

As I was telling Gavin some of the more graphic elements of my visions, I heard a polite cough behind me.

I stopped in mid-sentence and looked over my shoulder. A red-faced man was standing there. He must have heard my X-rated ramblings. My cheeks flooded with heat and I quickly looked away.

The man cleared his throat and said, "Mrs Booth? I'm DCI Parker. I want to speak to you about an accident involving Carmel Johnson. Is this a good time or have I interrupted something private?"

My head snapped back to the man. DCI Parker? No. It couldn't be. Of all the police officers in the world, not him!

Chapter 6

In that moment, DCI Sebastian Parker recognised me too. A friendly look came into his eyes. It swiftly vanished and was replaced with a cold one. I knew that look of old.

He said, "I didn't realise it was you, Karis. I didn't know you were married."

Gavin said, "She won't be, not for much longer." He gave me a pointed look and added, "I'll be in touch." He headed for his car, jumped in and zoomed away sending up a shower of gravel as he did so.

Sebastian Parker said, "Was I interrupting some sort of marital role play? I can come back another time."

"Role play? Of course it wasn't role play." I said brusquely. "I'm sorry you had to hear that language coming from me. I never talk like that. I didn't realise I knew so many rude words. I haven't seen you in a long time, Seb. How are you?"

"It's DCI Parker. Detective Chief Inspector Parker. I was told you have some information about Carmel. Before we continue, does that information have anything to do with your…" He stopped talking and raised his eyebrows.

"My psychic abilities? It's alright. You can say those words." I tried to keep the anger out of my voice. It was bad enough having Gavin feel this way about me, but to have a blast from the past joining in was too much for me today.

DCI Parker lifted his chin. "There's no need to take that tone with me, Mrs Booth. I'm here on official business. Answer my question."

I'd had enough of being spoken to in a condescending manner. I inserted my key into the lock and opened the door. I pushed it open and said, "I'll tell you everything inside. I'd rather not talk on the doorstep. You can come in and listen to me or you can clear off back to the police station."

I'd only walked a short way down the hallway before I heard footsteps behind me and then the sound of the door closing. I headed for the kitchen and switched the coffee maker on.

DCI Parker let out a low whistle and said, "You've done well for yourself, Karis. This kitchen is massive. How many bedrooms have you got?" He moved over to the window and gazed out. "Is that a swimming pool out there? Is it a heated one? It must be if it's outside."

I was surprised at his change in attitude, but I didn't say anything. I much preferred this version of him. He reminded me of the boy he used to be.

I added ground coffee to the maker and pressed a button. "Coffee?" I asked. "I'm having one. And, by the way, this house has six bedrooms. Oh, and it's got an indoor pool too."

DCI Parker whistled again and looked at me. "Wow. You have done well. Or is it your husband who's done well?"

"Why would it be my husband?" I asked. "That's a big assumption to make." He was right to a certain degree, but I wasn't going to correct him.

DCI Parker looked embarrassed and muttered, "Sorry. You're right; that was an assumption. No to coffee, thank you. I can't stay long." He moved away from the window and continued, "Tell me what you know about Carmel Johnson. Did you ever meet her?"

I quickly made myself a cup of coffee and then sat at the kitchen table. DCI Parker remained standing.

I told him everything. From meeting Carmel and the shadows behind her to the limited information her colleague, Travis, had given to Erin earlier today.

As expected, there was a look of disbelief on his face. I'd seen that look many times. People didn't believe a word I told them when it came to my visions. The disbelieving look was usually replaced by a sympathetic one. I knew what most people thought about me. They thought I was crazy and needed medical help. But I was past caring what anyone thought today.

I concluded with, "You can think what you like about my psychic abilities, but I trust them. I know Carmel was pushed. Her death wasn't an accident."

DCI Parker regarded me coolly. "Did you see her being pushed down a set of stairs?"

"No, but—"

"Did you see any signs of the building she was in?"

"No, but—"

He held his hand up. "You saw a shadow pushing Carmel Johnson. Is that right?"

"Yes, but—"

He said, "She could have been pushed at any time during the day. Whatever you think you saw could have had nothing to do with her death. Is that a reasonable assumption?"

I looked down at my coffee. "I suppose so. But I did get the feeling the second shadow was malicious in nature."

"A malicious shadow? Hmm. It's not much to go on, is it?"

I looked up sharply. "Not when you put it like that. Are you treating Carmel's death as an accident?"

"I'm not at liberty to say," he added loftily. "I'll see myself out. Goodbye, Mrs Booth."

I seethed as I cupped my hands around my coffee. I didn't know what had got into me lately, but the meek, feeble woman who'd put up with anything was gone. I didn't recognise this new version of myself, but it felt good. It was like I'd given myself permission to be who I was supposed to be. I liked it.

I said to the empty kitchen, "I'll prove it wasn't an accident. I'll prove Carmel Johnson was murdered."

How I was going to do that wasn't clear to me yet. I was hoping inspiration would dawn on me soon.

And it did. Before I'd finished my coffee, I knew what I had to do.

Chapter 7

I went straight over to Erin's house and told her about my visit from DCI Parker. She was sitting on the sofa with a blanket over her legs. Robbie was at her side and they were holding hands. It soothed my jaded heart to know some marriages survived. I sat in the chair opposite them as I told them about my conversation.

Erin said, "Sebastian Parker? From our street? The one you went to school with?"

I nodded. "The very same."

"And he's a DCI now?" Erin went on. She looked at Robbie. "Why didn't you tell us the investigating officer was Sebastian Parker? You should have warned Karis."

"I wasn't aware you both knew him," Robbie replied. "I've never heard you mention him."

Erin gave him a knowing look. "That's because we never talk about him. Not after the way he treated Karis."

"Oh?" Robbie's eyebrows rose. He shot an enquiring glance my way.

I said, "Let's not drag up the past."

Erin said, "Is he still handsome? I bet he is, the crafty thing. It'll be just like him to keep his looks."

I shrugged. "I didn't notice." I shrugged again. "I suppose he's aged well. He's got all his hair."

Erin gave me a small smile. "Do his brown eyes still twinkle with mischief when he talks? Does his mouth twitch as if he's going to break into a smile?"

"He didn't do any twinkling at me," I informed her. "And I don't recall him smiling. He frowned a lot and gave me dismissive looks."

"Maybe he was trying to hide his true feelings from you." Erin turned to Robbie. "Karis and Seb were a couple in their youth. He was mad about her."

"Oh?" Robbie turned his enquiring look to his wife now.

She flapped her hand at him. "Let's not rake up the past. We don't like Seb Parker, and we haven't for years. Not since the incident. Robbie, can't you talk to him and make him see sense about Karis' vision?"

Robbie shook his head. "I can't interfere in someone else's investigation."

"You don't have to interfere. Just tell him he's wrong and that Karis is right." Erin gave Robbie a bright smile as if that would convince him.

His smile was affectionate in return. "I can't do that, my sugar plum. Not even for you."

"Pah! Some husband you are." Erin shook her head and then winked at him.

"I've got a plan," I announced to them. "Robbie, I know Carmel fell down stairs at the factory. Do you know where those stairs are?" I paused. "You don't have to tell me if you're not legally able to."

"I can tell you. It's already been revealed online by the local press. It's the stairs that lead from the reception area and up to the offices. Before you ask, I don't know why Carmel was there or who she was visiting in the offices. I don't even know who works in those offices. You'd have to talk to DCI Parker about that."

Erin tutted. "Let's not mention his name again. Karis, why do you need to know that?"

"I thought I might visit the area where Carmel died and see if I can pick up on anything."

"Ooo. Interesting," Erin said. "What do you think you'll pick up on? Some image of the person who pushed her?"

"I don't know. I've never been involved in anything like this before. I've just got a feeling I should try to get some more information."

Erin nodded. "You should trust those feelings. You should go over there right now."

"I'm going to, but I need your help with something. I hope this isn't an awful thing to ask, but could you write a condolence card for Mr Nithercott at the factory? That would give me the perfect excuse to go there."

Erin smiled and looked at Robbie. "I told you it was a good idea to write that card, didn't I?"

"You did. I was going to post it later. I'll get it for you." Robbie stood up and headed towards the kitchen.

"I was going to send a card anyway," Erin explained. "But I had a feeling I should write it sooner rather than later. I must have known you'd need it. Perhaps I've got some psychic abilities too." She waggled her eyebrows at me and grinned.

I glanced towards the kitchen door and could hear Robbie singing to himself. I took the opportunity to say what was on my mind. "Erin, is everything alright with you?"

Erin blanched. "What do you mean? Of course everything is alright."

"I know it's my fault that I haven't been to the café for a while, but it was always busy when I went. It isn't like that anymore. Why?"

"Oh, you know what businesses are like. Busy one day and then quiet the next." Her smile didn't reach her eyes.

"Are you having problems with the café? Is there something I can do to help?"

"Things have been quiet lately, but I'm sure they'll pick up. Would you like a cup of tea?" She pulled the cover off her legs.

"What about your staff?"

"What staff?"

"Exactly. I haven't seen any at the café. You used to employ people. Where are they?"

Erin tried again to reassure me. "It's hard to get reliable staff these days. Would you like a biscuit to go with your tea?" She made a move to stand up.

Robbie came back into the room. "Stay right where you are, Mrs Terris. And put that blanket back over you. You're going nowhere, not after the shock you've had."

My senses picked up. I gave Robbie a sharp look. "What's wrong with Erin? What aren't you telling me?" I narrowed my eyes at him and mentally willed him to tell me the truth.

"You can stop squinting at me like that," Robbie said. "There's nothing wrong with your sister apart from her working too hard. She needs to take it easy for a while." He handed me an envelope. "Here's the card of condolence. Now, listen to me carefully. Don't interfere with this police enquiry. If you have a vision while you're at the factory, let DCI Parker know."

Erin said loudly, "We're not talking to him."

Robbie went on, "Or you could tell me. Let me walk you to the door."

I gave Erin a quick hug before I left. I had a lot of hugs to catch up on.

Robbie walked me to my car and as I opened it, he glanced back at the house before saying quietly, "Karis, see what you can do about this Carmel thing. It's upset Erin greatly and I don't like to see her like this." He looked as if he were going to say a lot more, but then he stopped.

"Robbie, is Erin okay? You would let me know if she's not, wouldn't you?"

"Of course. She's fine." He held the car door open for me. "You take care now. If you sense any danger at all in that factory, get the hell out of there and come back here. Understand?"

"I do." I gave him a searching look in the hope of picking up on whatever was bothering him.

He laughed and said, "You'll give yourself wrinkles if you keep squinting like that." He closed the car door and walked back to the house.

I stared at the house for a while. Those two were keeping something from me. Why couldn't I switch my psychic powers on when I needed them?

I shook my head at myself. Maybe it was something I didn't need to know right now. I started the car and set off in the direction of the Nithercott factory. I knew in the pit of my stomach that something was going to happen to me there.

Chapter 8

Luck wasn't on my side as I pulled into the factory car park a short while later. DCI Parker was standing next to a black car and facing the car park entrance. He kept his eyes on me as I manoeuvred my car into the last remaining space. Unfortunately, that space was right where he was standing and I had to give him a polite hand gesture to get him to move. He did so reluctantly and then waited for me to get out of my car.

"Mrs Booth," he began in that cold tone of his, "what are you doing here?"

I held up Erin's card. "I'm here to deliver this condolence card on behalf of my sister. She's been doing business with Mr Nithercott for years. Is that against the law?"

His eyes narrowed. "Why didn't she post it?"

"Because she's not well."

The suspicion on his face lifted. "Isn't she? I'm sorry to hear that. I haven't seen Erin for years. How is she?"

"Fine." I gave him a suspicious look. "Can you stop going hot and cold on me? It's confusing."

"Hot and cold? I don't understand your meaning, Mrs Booth."

I wagged the envelope at him. "One minute you're acting like we're old friends, and the next you're treating me like a common criminal who's got something to hide."

"Have you? Something to hide? What's in that envelope? Did your sister really write it? Or is it a coded letter to Mr Nithercott telling him about your vision?"

I gave him a blank look. "I never thought of doing that. Erin did write it. She knew Carmel and liked her a lot. She's upset over Carmel's death and the least I can do is hand over this condolence card on her behalf. I don't see any problem with that."

He held his hand out. "I can take it for you. I'm going to talk to Mr Nithercott now."

I pulled the envelope out of his reach. "Erin wants me to deliver it. It wouldn't be the same coming from you."

"You can't talk to him at the moment. I've made an appointment to speak to him."

"What about?"

"None of your business, Mrs Booth. I suggest you go home and come back another time."

I leaned as casually as I could against my car. "I'm not going anywhere. I'll wait here all day until Mr Nithercott comes out if I have to." The smell of baking bread caught on a breeze and wafted towards me. My stomach growled in appreciation.

DCI Parker's mouth twitched at one corner. He raised his finger in my direction. "You're dribbling. It's not a good look."

I used the back of my hand to wipe my mouth. "I can't help it! It's the smell of fresh bread."

He let out the smallest of chuckles and looked away.

"Oh, shut up," I mumbled under my breath.

He looked back at me. "That's no way to talk to an officer of the law." He studied me for a moment which made me feel uneasy. What was his problem?

He clicked his fingers and said, "You're up to something. I can see it on your face. You want to talk to Mr Nithercott on your own. You want to find out more about Carmel Johnson. Aha! I know your game, Karis. Erm, Mrs Booth."

I truthfully said, "I wasn't planning on doing that at all."

"You can't fool me. You can go and see Mr Nithercott now, but I'm coming with you. Try anything funny and you'll regret it. I'm dealing with an investigation and I won't have you messing things up."

I pushed my luck and said, "A murder investigation?"

"None of your business." He moved to one side. "After you, Mrs Booth."

I shot him a filthy look but it was wasted as he wasn't even looking at me. He was right behind me as I walked into the factory and over to the reception desk. He didn't even give me the chance to speak to the kind-faced man sitting behind the reception desk.

DCI said to the man, "DCI Parker. Here to see Mr Nithercott. I have an appointment."

The man checked a book in front of him, smiled up at DCI Parker and said, "Yes, Mr Nithercott is expecting you. Up the stairs and it's the first door on the left. Would you like a complimentary box of mini loaves?" He pushed a large basket of delectable looking gift boxes towards the chief inspector.

"No." DCI turned on his heel and walked towards the stairs.

I gave the man an apologetic smile and said, "I'm Karis. Your company supplies bread to my sister's café. We've heard about Carmel's untimely death. We're so sorry. I only met her once, but she seemed lovely."

The man gave me a wobbly smile and nodded. "She was. We're all devastated. The place won't be the same without her. She'd only been here a few months, but she was so energetic and full of life. She had so many wonderful ideas for the company too."

I could feel the sadness coming from him in waves. I said, "And how are you coping?"

"As well as I can. I have to keep going for Mr Nithercott's sake. Would you like a box of mini loaves?"

"I would love some. Thank you. That's very kind." I took one of the boxes and put it in my handbag. I pulled out a fresh pack of tissues and handed them to the man. "Just in case you need them."

He gave me a grateful smile.

I nearly jumped out of my skin as DCI Parker barked, "Mrs Booth! This way. Please."

He was standing on the third step up and waiting for me.

I refrained from rolling my eyes at the impatient police officer and walked towards him. The stairs were wide enough for two people to walk side by side, so that's what DCI Parker did. He matched my every step up with his own. It was like he was frightened I'd make a run for it and race into Mr Nithercott's office before him.

We entered Mr Nithercott's office together and found him sitting behind a large, wooden desk. He was an elderly man and his suit was what my late grandma would describe as "dapper." His tie and pocket square complimented the dark blue of his suit. His eyes were red-rimmed and there was a box of tissues in front of him. I could almost touch the grief which surrounded him.

Before DCI Parker could stop me, I walked towards Mr Nithercott and placed my hand on his arm. "Hello, I'm Karis. You supply goods to my sister, Erin Terris. We're so sorry for your loss."

He patted my hand. "I know Erin. She's been one of my clients for years. Carmel said Erin liked the new recipes. Is that right? Did she? I'm not one for change, but Carmel was all for it. She was a forward-thinker. Such ideas. Such ambition." His gaze dropped. "All gone."

DCI Parker said, "Mrs Booth has brought you a condolence card." He gave me a pointed look.

I placed the card on the desk.

Mr Nithercott looked at me and said, "That's kind of you. I believe Travis will be taking over Carmel's delivery route now." There was a fraction of a pause. "Let me know if Erin has any problems with him."

"I will do. Please let us know when the funeral is. We'd like to be there."

DCI Parker opened the office door wide. "Mrs Booth, you may go now."

I shot him a dark look which he caught this time and his eyes widened. There was no need for him to be so rude.

I left the office and headed for the stairs. I stopped and looked around to make sure no one was there. Then I concentrated on what I'd felt on the way up the stairs. I knew I was going to receive a vision of Carmel's recent past. I steadied myself against the wall and waited.

Chapter 9

The vision began.

I could hear something; the sound of someone breathing. I put my hand on the handrail and felt it vibrating. I let my focus soften.

There she was. Carmel Johnson. Standing on the top step inches away from me. She had her back to me but I could hear her heavy breathing. She was furious about something. Some injustice. I felt it strongly. My eyes smarted as I tried not to cry. I saw Carmel move her hand to her face and wipe something away. Tears?

What was that smell? It was something familiar. Smoke of some sort, but not cigarette smoke. It was sweeter.

A voice called out Carmel's name. It sounded like it was underwater and I couldn't say if it was a man or a woman's voice.

Carmel looked over her shoulder. I saw the bitterness on her face as she recognised the person who'd called her name. Her right hand was resting on her lower abdomen and I felt a flicker of something in my stomach. It felt like butterflies.

Carmel shook her head vehemently at the unknown person and turned her head back. She took a step downwards.

That's when it happened. Hands shot out and pushed Carmel with a determined force. Carmel yelped with shock.

Then she fell. I could hear every sickening thump as her body rolled down the steps.

I instinctively reached out to stop her and cried, "No!"

She landed at the bottom of the stairs with her face looking upwards. I saw her eyes flutter before they closed forever. I whipped my head around to see if her killer was there.

DCI Sebastian Parker was standing there. His face was solemn and his eyes bore into mine. His voice was husky as he said, "Karis, what just happened? You're crying. What did you see?"

I dashed my tears away. "I saw everything. I saw Carmel fall to her death. I know you don't believe in my visions, but I saw her." My voice cracked and I took a second to compose myself. I placed my hand on my lower abdomen just as Carmel had done. "She was pregnant. I felt it here."

DCI Parker gave me an incredulous look. "That's impossible. How could you feel that?"

"I don't know, I just do!" My voice rose. "I've just witnessed a murder. I don't care whether you believe me or not. I saw someone push her. Someone was standing right where you were."

"Did you see who it was?"

"No. I turned around to have a look and saw you instead." I looked back at the bottom of the stairs. "She was all crumpled up like a rag doll. That poor girl. And her poor baby."

DCI Parker said, "Karis, I don't know what to do with this information. I'd like to believe you, but..." his voice trailed off.

I gave him a small smile. "But your sensible mind won't let you. I understand. But you can find out if she was pregnant, can't you? That could be relevant to her death. Don't you think?"

He gave me a long look before saying, "Yes, it could be. I'll see what I can do. Go home and get some rest. If what you say is true, then you've had a tremendous shock."

I was too distraught to argue with him over the truth of my vision. I kept my hand on the handrail as I walked down the steps. Instinctively, I gave the area where Carmel had landed a wide berth. I could feel DCI Parker looking at me, but I didn't give him a backward glance as I left the factory.

I got into my car and looked at the building. Someone killed Carmel Johnson in there. Those visions about her were coming to me for some reason. The guilt over Robbie's shooting came back to me. I should have done a lot more to help him and to prevent that incident. I couldn't change the past, but I was going to make sure I did everything I could to help Carmel.

Chapter 10

I went straight back to Erin's house as I wanted to share my psychic experience with her. I could always rely on my sister to take my visions seriously.

Erin answered the door to me, took one look at my face and said, "You need a strong cup of tea. Come in. Robbie's nipped out to the supermarket."

Once we were settled with a cup of tea in the living room, I told Erin everything.

She shook her head sadly. "That's awful. Just awful. Poor you having to see that. Can you remember anything else about the person who pushed her? Did they have a young voice or an old one?"

"I couldn't make it out. I've been going over and over it. You don't think it was Mr Nithercott, do you? He's got an office near the stairs."

"Why would he do that?"

I gave her a look. "Perhaps he's the father of her child."

"But he's two hundred years old!" Erin exclaimed. She gave me a cheeky grin. "Although, if there's still lead in the pencil…"

I shuddered. "Don't complete that sentence. How well did you know Carmel?"

"Not very well. We only managed to exchange a few words each time she delivered the bread. But she was one of those people who you warm to immediately. She was so genuine. She cared what my customers thought about Nithercott's products. She cared what I thought too. I know she was behind a lot of the new recipes. She had a knack for knowing about changing trends. From the small things she let slip, I don't think everyone was happy with her new recipes."

I settled back in the sofa with my cup snuggled in my hands. "Tell me more."

"It's that man she worked with — Travis. Like I told you earlier, he used to deliver my bread. The miserable so-and-so. From what I gathered, he wasn't happy about Carmel taking over his route."

"Why not?"

"I think it had something to do with all the customers on my route being close together. It didn't take long to deliver bread to us all. Travis' new route takes him longer as his customers are more spread out. I know he didn't like the new recipes and told his customers they had nothing to do with him. He encouraged them to make complaints. And that's what they did. Mr Nithercott got many complaints from people on Travis' route."

"Did Carmel tell you this?"

Erin nodded. "She was upset one day which was unusual, so I insisted she tell me what was wrong. She told me how Travis had got his customers to complain about the bread. He'd also bad-mouthed her at the factory and said she was after Mr Nithercott's job. He'd really upset her with his malicious rumours." Erin's eyes narrowed. "I can just imagine Travis doing something like that."

"When did Carmel tell you this?"

"A few weeks ago. She was back to her usual happy self the day after and didn't mention Travis again." She gave me a considered look. "Do you think it was Travis who pushed her down the stairs?"

"I don't know. What do you think?"

Erin said, "I think he'd do something like that. He's nasty enough. He's the one who found her at the bottom of the stairs, so that puts him at the crime scene."

"What's all this talk about a crime scene?" Robbie came into the room. "I've only been gone for thirty minutes and you're trying to take over my job. Hello, Karis. Are you staying for lunch? I'm going to put the shopping away and then make something for my crime-fighting wife."

A call of hello came from the kitchen.

"Ah," Robbie said as he ran his hand across the back of his neck. "Guess who I saw at the supermarket?"

An elderly woman in a tartan coat ambled into the living room. She beamed at us and declared, "It's only me. Robbie said you were here Karis, and I thought I'd pop in and say hello. "

"Peggy!" I put my cup down, got to my feet and went over to the woman. She was smaller than me by a foot so I had to lean down to hug her. As always, she smelled of roses.

I'd known Peggy Marshall all my life. She'd been Mum's next door neighbour for years. They'd moved into their houses within a week of each other and had become firm friends immediately. Peggy was like a second mum to Erin and me. She was kind-hearted and looked on the bright side of life. She was one of those people who lifted your spirits every time you met her.

She was also the nosiest person in the world. She knew everything about everyone.

Once I'd released Peggy, she looked me up and down and announced, "Karis Booth, you look better than you have in years. It's not my place to say this, but I'm glad you're getting a divorce. That Gavin Booth is one of the worst humans I've ever met. He sucked the life and ambition right out of you. He's like one of those emotional vampires. I saw a programme on the telly about them and I thought to myself that they're just like Gavin Booth."

"How did you know about my divorce?" I asked. The second the words were out of my mouth, I knew it was a silly question.

"I saw Henry at the butcher's. His granddaughter works at the sandwich shop near the solicitors in town. She saw you going in there and mentioned it to Carol who she works with and she said—"

I held my hand up. "I shouldn't have asked you that. I know you have friends all over this town. Nothing gets past you."

Erin noted, "Peggy, you're like the human equivalent of Google."

Peggy gave her a grin. "Erin, how are you? You look peaky."

Erin flashed her a bright smile. "I'm fine. Really fine."

Peggy gave her a look which said she didn't believe her. She went on, "I won't keep you. I hope you don't mind me saying this, Erin, but your mum's garden needs some attention. The weeds are running riot. And her windows are becoming a disgrace. Would you like me to sort it out? I don't mind. I've got a spare key."

Erin replied, "No, thank you. I'm sorry Mum's house is like that. I haven't managed to get round there recently. I've been too busy with work."

I looked at Erin. "I didn't know you were looking after Mum's house. How long have you been doing that? Why didn't you let me know? I could have helped."

Erin looked away from my gaze.

Peggy said, "She's been doing it since your mum went into the care home. She couldn't tell you on account of you two not talking to each other." She looked at Robbie. "But they've got that sorted out now, haven't they?"

Robbie nodded. "They have. At last."

Peggy continued, "Aye, but I'll bet you my last packet of bath salts that Karis still feels bad about you getting shot." She turned her knowing eyes on me. "You do, don't you? There's no point feeling bad. It wasn't your fault. It was that emotional vampire, Gavin Booth. He never supported you and your gifts. Never." She put her hand on my arm. "He couldn't see how special you were. He never appreciated your gift. You're still getting those pictures in your head. You had a vision of that poor lass at the bread factory."

"How do you know that?"

Robbie blurted out, "I told her. I couldn't help it! She wheedled the truth out of me. She should work for MI6."

Peggy chuckled. "I wouldn't be cut out for that sort of work. I like my home comforts too much. Speaking of which, Robbie, would you mind giving me a lift to the bus stop? There's a bus due in five minutes and I'm not sure my legs will make it with all the shopping I've got."

"Course I will," Robbie replied. "When I've dropped you off, I'll call into Lorena's house and give it a good going-over."

I made a decision and said, "No, you won't. I'll do it. It's about time I did my fair share concerning Mum's house. Peggy, I'll give you a lift home. Where are your shopping bags?"

"I've left them in the kitchen. Thank you, Karis. We can have a good natter in the car."

That's exactly what I was counting on. I said goodbye to Erin and Robbie and promised I'd phone them later.

I took Peggy's bags to my car and put them in the boot. Peggy settled herself in the passenger seat with her handbag on her lap.

As soon as we drove away, she said to me, "Right, what do you want to talk about first? The murder of that lass? Or the secrets Erin and Robbie are keeping from you?"

Chapter 11

"Let's start with Erin and Robbie," I said. "What's going on with them?"

"I was hoping you'd tell me that with you being psychic and all. Have you had any visions about them? Any premonitions? Overheard any secret conversations?"

I shot Peggy a quick glance. "No, I haven't. I can't switch my abilities on and off. I wish I could."

"You should go to one of those spiritual churches. I've seen them advertised in the paper. They do psychic development classes. I've clipped the advert out and kept it in my kitchen drawer. I thought it might come in useful for you one day."

"Perhaps. All I've picked up on from those two is that they're keeping something from me. I think it's something to do with Erin's health."

Peggy said, "Aye, that explains it. She hasn't been working full-time at the café. She keeps taking time off. And she's laid her staff off. I thought her and Robbie were having money problems and had decided to cut down on staff. But if there's something wrong with her health, then she would want to cut her hours down." She paused for a few seconds. "What do you think is wrong with her?"

Unease settled in my stomach. "I don't know. I hope it's nothing serious. Like…" I stopped. I was not going to finish that sentence.

Peggy reached over and patted my hand. "Let's not worry about things that aren't there. Erin could simply be cutting down on her hours and doing something else. That café of hers isn't as busy as it used to be. I expect it's the competition. There are two new cafés in town now and they do all sorts of fancy food. They're not to my liking, but some people like it. Why don't you sit her down for a serious talk and get to the bottom of it? I'd like to know what's wrong with her too."

I caught the worry in her voice and said, "I will do."

Peggy didn't have children of her own. Erin and I were the closest to a family she had.

We arrived at the semi-detached houses which Mum and Peggy owned. Even as I pulled up to Mum's house, I could see the dust on the windows and the foot-high weeds in the garden. Mum's house was a stark contrast to Peggy's next door. Her house positively gleamed with cleanliness.

I sighed as I switched the car engine off. "I'm sorry about Mum's house. I'll get it cleaned up."

"I know you will. You don't have to do it this very second. Help me in with my shopping and I'll make you a ham and cheese sandwich. As usual, I've bought too much. I know my Jeff's been gone three years now, but I keep shopping for two. That's the problem with losing someone so close to you; you keep forgetting they're gone."

I insisted on carrying Peggy's shopping bags into her kitchen. Like the rest of the house, it was spotless. It had a wonderfully welcoming feel to it. It was like the house was opening its arms and giving me a hug.

I put Peggy's shopping away while she made us some lunch.

As soon as we sat at the kitchen table, Peggy said, "Let me tell you what I know about that bakery lass, Carmel. I never met her, but I know plenty who did. Lovely girl she was by all accounts. Always inventing new bread with fancy bits in them. I know about that shifty man who worked with her. Travis, he's called. He hated Carmel from the minute she started working for Mr Nithercott. Eat up, Karis."

I picked my sandwich up. "I will. Why did Travis hate Carmel?"

"Because she was a conscientious worker. She turned up early to work and stayed late. She did her deliveries on time and talked to each of her customers to make sure they were happy with the deliveries. Not like Travis. He couldn't care less about his customers or the bread. He got up a petition, you know. He didn't like that new loaf that Carmel had worked on. He got his customers to sign a petition to get rid of the new recipe, and to get rid of Carmel."

I lowered my sandwich, "Did he? What was his reason?"

"He claimed Carmel was messing with a tried and tested recipe. Some people liked the original Nithercott classic loaf. They didn't want change. But I know the majority loved the new recipe and they wouldn't sign his petition. It wouldn't surprise me if Travis forged their signatures."

"What was he going to do with his petition?"

"He was going to take it to Mr Nithercott. Perhaps he was hoping Mr Nithercott would fire Carmel."

I gave her a slow nod. "What if Travis did that yesterday? And what if Mr Nithercott refused to fire Carmel? Travis could have seen her on the stairs and pushed her in a fit of rage." I put my half-eaten sandwich down. "But that doesn't explain her feelings. She felt angry at someone before she fell. She wanted to get justice."

Peggy frowned. "How do you know that? Oh, you had another vision. Robbie told me you were going to the bread factory. Tell me everything."

I did so.

Peggy nodded. "Carmel could have been annoyed with Travis. Let's say he took his petition to Mr Nithercott. Then Mr Nithercott spoke to Carmel later and showed her the petition. That would have been enough to rattle her."

"Yes, but why would Travis then push her down the steps?"

Peggy shrugged. "Because he's a nasty, little rat of a man. You should talk to him. See what you can pick up. I don't mean to be rude, Karis, but can you hurry up, please? I'm going to see your mum soon and the bus to the care home only runs once an hour. I don't want to miss it."

I picked my sandwich up. "I'll drive you there. I'll spend some time with Mum too."

"But it's not the second Sunday of the month," Peggy said. "You only see her on the second Sunday."

My glanced dropped downwards. "That was Gavin's suggestion. He said it was a waste of time going more often as Mum never recognised me. He said it so many times that I was convinced it was true." I looked at Peggy. "I've been such an idiot about him. I've been an utter and complete fool."

"You're not the only woman to say that about a man. Forget about Gavin Booth. He's out of your life for good. The nincompoop. Let's see your mum, and after that, we'll track down that Travis fella. We'll get the truth out of him."

"Shouldn't we leave this to the police?" I suggested.

"Do you mean that old friend of yours, Seb Parker? He's changed since he went to London. He's gone all hard faced. Robbie told me what Seb had said to you earlier when he went to your house. No, we won't leave this to that cold-hearted Seb Parker. We're going to find out who killed Carmel ourselves. Eat up."

Chapter 12

Mum had been at Wood Crescent Care Home for the last two years. Everything had fallen apart two years ago. Robbie had been shot and Dad had died shortly afterwards. Mum couldn't cope with the grief and she fell to pieces. Having lost her own husband the previous year, Peggy helped Mum through the grieving process, but it was soon clear that Mum wasn't just grieving. I remember the phone calls from Peggy telling me she'd found Mum wandering around the supermarket in her nightdress. Peggy had also discovered Mum doing gardening in the middle of the night and singing loudly to herself. I'd witnessed one of Mum's turns, and knew it was nothing to do with losing Dad. After difficult conversations with Erin and Robbie, we decided this care home would be the best place for her.

Wood Crescent Care Home had glowing reviews, and the staff genuinely cared for the patients. Even though it had broken my heart to do so, I was content as I could be at leaving Mum here. Her prospects of returning home were slim, but there was never any question of selling Mum's house. Even though we'd never voiced our opinions to each other, Erin and I considered Mum's stay here to be a temporary one. The thought of her not returning home, and back to her former self, was too hard for us to contemplate. So we didn't. I knew deep down that we were fooling ourselves.

The woman on the reception desk gave us a cheery wave as we entered. A delicious smell of fish and chips wafted towards us.

Peggy explained, "They always have fish and chips on a Tuesday. Every week without fail. These old folk like their routines. Why don't you talk to Lorena first? I've got some other people to talk to here. I'll catch up with you in a bit."

She wandered off down the corridor raising her hand in greeting to many people.

I headed towards the Sun Room where Mum spent most of her time. Huge windows overlooked the beautiful gardens and Mum loved to stare out at the trees.

She wasn't the only quiet one who stared out of the windows. I spotted three other residents gazing out while their loved ones sat opposite them with overly bright smiles on their faces as they tried to make conversation.

I walked over to Mum and sat in the chair opposite her. I said gently, "Mum, it's me, Karis."

Mum turned her attention away from the window and gave me a quizzical look. Then she gave me a polite smile, the kind you'd give to a stranger. Even though I was used to it, it still hurt. Mum turned her head back to the view outside.

I persevered, "Mum, I know this isn't my usual day for visiting, but Peggy was coming so I thought I'd tag along with her. Lorrie is doing well in her new job. You remember Lorrie, don't you? Your granddaughter. I told you last time she'd started working for that online protection company." I let out a laugh. "She's not allowed to talk about her job and even had to sign some official papers about confidentiality and all that. When I ask her about her job, she looks as if she's fit to burst with all the information she's come across. You know how bad she is at keeping secrets! I'm not entirely sure it's the best career choice for her, but she loves it."

Mum's attention went to a robin on the grass outside the window. The corner of her mouth lifted slightly as she watched the bird's antics.

I carried on, "I've got a bit of news too, Mum. I've decided to get a divorce. I thought it was about time I came to my senses." I couldn't help but give a hollow laugh. "About time too, you're thinking. I know you never liked Gavin."

Mum turned her head back to me. She gave me such a sharp look that it took my breath away.

Her voice was hoarse as she said, "Gavin? Gone? For good?"

Had she actually understood me?

I nodded. "Yes, Gavin's gone for good."

She lifted a thin hand and held it out to me. She croaked, "Good. I'm happy."

I reached out for her hand. As soon as I did so, an image flashed into my head of Mum and me playing in the garden. It was so real. I could hear our laughter and feel the sun on my bare shoulders. I must have been about nine or ten.

I looked into Mum's eyes and smiled.

She smiled back and said, "Garden. I remember. I can hear you laughing."

"Me too, Mum."

We continued to hold hands and the image of us in the garden intensified. I could even taste the strawberry ice cream which Mum bought for me from the ice cream van.

Tears of happiness rolled down my cheeks as the image continued. It was like being inside a TV show. The colours were so bright and the noises so clear. Unlike a TV show, I could experience the smells too. It was wonderful, even magical.

Mum squeezed my hand and said, "A good day, Karis, a good day. I remember it well. Gavin's gone? For good?"

I nodded, unable to speak. Mum hadn't said this many words since she'd moved into the care home.

Mum gave my hand a final squeeze and said, "Good. I'm glad. He's a nincompoop. I'm tired." She took her hand back and rested it on her lap. Her eyes closed and the smallest of smiles alighted on her lips.

I wiped my tears away.

Peggy appeared at my side. "Karis? Why are you crying? Is she dead? Is Lorena dead? Don't tell me she's passed on!"

I stood up and told Peggy what had happened. I concluded, "It was only a few minutes, but I felt as if I had her back with me. I think she felt it too."

Peggy smiled. "You're a lucky girl to experience that. It must be your psychic powers coming out more now that you're away from that joy-sucking vampire. Mind you, your mum had her psychic moments too. Whatever it was that you just experienced, I'm pleased for you."

We both looked at Mum who was now asleep. She looked peaceful.

I ventured, "Do you think the mum I know is still in there? In her head?"

"She could be. There's no harm in thinking that. I would say don't get your hopes up, but why shouldn't you? That's what hopes are for. Raise them as high as you can. Why don't you have a walk outside in the gardens? It's lovely out there. I'll keep an eye on your mum."

I was about to say no, but then a familiar smell came towards me. It was the scent of that smoke I'd inhaled during my visit to the bread factory. Where was it coming from?

An elderly man in a tweed jacket walked past me and the smell increased. I could see a pipe sticking out from his top pocket.

I whispered to Peggy, "Who's that? I've seen him here before, but I don't know his name."

"That's Cyril. Cyril Simpson. He comes here to see his wife, Maggie. Why do you want to know who he is?

Have you just had a funny feeling about him? Is he going to kick the bucket soon?"

"No. I think he was at the bread factory earlier. That smoky smell is coming from him. Now I know why it was so familiar. I've smelled it before when I've been to visit Mum. It must linger on his clothes."

Peggy looked at Cyril as he left the room. "What was he doing at the bread factory? Don't just stand there, Karis, get after him!"

Chapter 13

I followed Cyril out of the building and into the garden. He walked to the nearest bench, sat down and put his head in his hands. I hated to intrude on such a private moment, but I had to.

"Erm. Excuse me. Sorry for bothering you. I'm Karis Booth."

Cyril looked up at me and my heart twisted at the grief on his lined face. "Yes? What do you want? Have I left something behind? I'm always doing that lately." He squinted. "I've seen you before. Aren't you Lorena's oldest? I didn't know you worked here."

"I don't." I took a seat. I looked at him for a moment. How was I supposed to explain that I'd smelled him in a vision? It sounded weird even to me.

Cyril straightened up and sat back on the bench. He said, "It's so sad, isn't it? To see my Maggie and your mum like that. They're the people we've known and loved for so long, but they're not really there. I wonder what they think about? Do you suppose they still have memories?"

I gave him a slow nod. "I suppose they might. Even if they're only small memories."

"I hope they do. I hope Maggie remembers something about her life however small." He blinked rapidly. "Anyway, enough about me. Did you want to talk to me about something?"

"I did. This is going to sound really strange, but have you been to the Nithercott bread factory recently?"

Cyril gave me a wide-eyed stare. "It's those CCTV cameras! They follow your every movement. It's like living in a fishbowl! Is that where you work? Did old Mr Nithercott send you here to tell me not to go back? Well, you can tell him from me that I won't be going back! And not one morsel of his disgusting bread will pass over my lips again. Never!"

I wasn't expecting such an outburst. "I don't work for Mr Nithercott."

"I don't blame you. He's a disgrace to the bread profession. Changing his recipe like that! No respect for his loyal customers. Why are companies so keen to improve everything these days? Why can't they leave stuff alone? I loved Nithercott bread. The old one, not the new one. That's why I went there. To let him know how I felt. I'm sure I'm not the only one."

"What did you say to Mr Nithercott?"

"I told him how I felt. He was very nice about it and offered me some free loaves as compensation. But it was something with sunflower seeds in it. Seeds in a loaf? Can you believe that? What's the world coming to? I told him he wasn't being fair to his loyal customers and he should continue to bake the old bread. He said he couldn't and that he had to move along with the times. He said the old bread had too much salt in it and young people don't like that now." He shook his head sorrowfully.

An image came to me while he was talking. I saw a young couple inside a café. The man had a striking resemblance to Cyril, and he even had a pipe sticking out of his top pocket. From the clothes and surroundings, I could tell the image was from a long time ago.

I said gently, "Did your Maggie like the old recipe too?"

Cyril's wrinkly face broke into a smile. "She did. Nithercott's bread has a special place in our hearts." He waved his hand at me. "You don't want to hear about that. You've probably got something important to do."

"I haven't. I would love to hear more about you and Maggie."

"Okay. You asked for it." Cyril took his pipe out, looked at it and then put it back in his pocket. "Maggie used to work at a top-end department store in Harrogate. I fell for her the second I saw her. I was desperate to talk to her, but she worked in the perfume department and I didn't have an excuse to go over to her. I admired her from afar. She caught me staring at her one day and waved at me. She beckoned me over and asked if I had a woman in my life. I said yes, I had my mum. Maggie gave me a free sample of lilac perfume to give to my mum. She said I had to promise to return the following week and to let her know what Mum thought."

"That's a good chat-up line," I said with a smile.

Cyril grinned. "She was a bit of a minx was Maggie. Anyway, I went back time and time again. Maggie couldn't keep giving me free samples, so I paid for the cheapest items I could. I wasn't making much money then, but I was happy to spend it all at Maggie's counter. Mum loved our courtship days because she ended up with lots of perfumed products.

"I finally gathered my courage and invited Maggie out. To my amazement, she said yes. I took her to a posh café where they had tablecloths and waitresses." He tapped his pocket where his pipe was. "I even bought this so that I'd look grown-up and refined. That café was so posh that our sandwiches had their crusts removed! I don't know why they did that; the crust is the best bit. I kept my mouth shut, though. If that's how posh people eat their bread, who was I to argue?"

"Indeed," I said.

"The bread they served us was Nithercott's, the classic loaf. It had only just come out then and it was hard to find it in the local shops. Maggie loved it. And I loved it because she did. It became our thing. We stayed loyal to Nithercott's bread throughout our lives. We even had those posh sandwiches at our wedding!"

I gave him a nod. "I can understand why you're so upset about the new bread."

"It's not just the past memories of the bread," Cyril explained. "Ever since Maggie's been in here, her memory has got worse and worse. The only thing that got any reaction from her were the sandwiches I brought her. I made them specially with the crusts cut off. When she took a bite, I'd see a spark in her eyes like she was remembering something. It was my old Maggie. I know it was." He sighed heavily. "I took her some of the new bread yesterday. She didn't even touch it. She gave it one look and then stared out of the window. I lived for that spark in her eyes, and now it's gone. It's all Mr Nithercott's fault."

"I'm so sorry about that. Is there anything I could do to help?"

He gave me a wry smile. "You could convince Mr Nithercott to make the old bread again."

"I might just do that. When you were at the factory, did you see a young woman?" I described Carmel to him.

"Yes, I did. I was coming out of Mr Nithercott's office and heading for the stairs. I saw her coming up. She caught my eye as she had a look of Maggie about her. She gave me a lovely smile and bounded up the steps." Faint spots of colour came to his cheeks. "I did turn around and watch her as she walked away. Don't tell Maggie that."

"I won't. Where did the woman go?"

"She carried on down the corridor towards some doors. She went inside one of them and I heard—" He stopped abruptly. "No, I shouldn't say."

I said, "You can tell me."

"I heard a man shouting at her. Then I heard a woman shouting back. It must have been the young woman."

"Did you hear what they were saying?"

64

"He was saying something about her going too far, and then something about her ruining his plans. She yelled back that he needed to grow up. She sounded furious. I don't like people shouting at each other, so I quickly left." He pulled his pipe out and gave it a quizzical look. "I keep forgetting I've run out of tobacco. My local shop has stopped selling it. First, it's my bread, and now it's my tobacco. This world is getting too hard for me to deal with."

I picked up on his despair. I couldn't leave him like this. I said, "Have you looked online for the tobacco?"

"Online? You mean that internet thing? No, I haven't. I don't trust that internet."

I took my phone out. "Do you know the name of it?"

"Course I do. I've been buying it for years." He gave me the name and I tapped it into my phone.

I held my phone towards him. "Look, you can get it from this online shop. They'll deliver it to you."

"Will they?" His eyebrows shot up so much that they almost left his forehead.

I nodded. "I can order it for you. I've already got an account with this retailer. If you give me your address, I can make sure it goes there."

"Really? You will? How kind. How will I pay for it?"

"You won't. I will. It's my treat. And when you run out, you can phone me and I'll sort some more out for you. I'll give you my number."

Cyril's eyes welled up. "That's so very kind. I don't know what to say." He gave me his address. "Just order a small packet. Thank you."

I ordered him two of the larger packets. I wrote down my number for him and then we chatted for a few more minutes.

At one point, Cyril frowned and said, "Why did you ask me about going to the bread factory? You never did explain that."

I was saved from answering that question as Peggy came over to us. She said, "Karis, your mum is still asleep. I think we should go now. Hi, Cyril. How are you?"

"Hello, Peggy. I'm keeping well. You?"

"I can't complain, Cyril, I can't complain. See you later."

We walked back to the car, and when we got in, Peggy looked at me eagerly and said, "I know where we can find Travis. Let's go and interrogate him."

Chapter 14

A short while later I said to Peggy, "I've never been to a pub at this time of the afternoon before. Are you sure Travis will be here?"

Peggy nodded. "According to my sources, this is where he goes when he's finished his deliveries for the day. Once he's finished, he takes the van back to the factory, catches the number twenty-two bus and comes straight here. He only does this on Tuesdays, Wednesdays, and Thursdays." She frowned. "I'm not sure where he goes on Mondays and Fridays. I'll ask my sources about that. It might be relevant to our investigation."

I shook my head at her. "You really are a mine of information."

Peggy's eyes twinkled. "You'd be a mine of information too if you spoke to as many people as I do."

We went into the pub and over to the bar. I got myself an orange juice, and Peggy said she could manage a small gin and tonic. As neither Peggy nor I knew what Travis looked like, we asked the woman behind the bar if he was in.

She seemed surprised at our request and pointed to a corner of the pub. "Are you his friends? I didn't know he had any friends. There he is, sitting in his usual spot. There's something a bit different about him today. He's barely uttered a word since he came in. He normally complains non-stop the second he enters. Woe betide anyone who gets within hearing distance of his complaints. Travis is a man who thrives on complaining about anything and everything." She passed our drinks over to me and I paid her.

I said to the woman, "What does he complain about the most?"

"His workplace, of course. The big question is if he hates it so much, why does he still work there? That's what I've asked him when I've been unlucky enough to be near when he complains. He told me the shifts fit in with his lifestyle." She cast a sorrowful look in Travis' direction and added, "It's not much of a lifestyle. He goes to the factory, does his shift and then comes here for most of the evening. Still, you can't tell some people what's best for them, can you?"

Peggy replied, "Indeed not."

As we walked away from the bar, Peggy said to me quietly, "If we're going to get some information from Travis, let me try reverse psychology on him. I saw a programme on the telly about that. I know what to say and do. Follow my lead. If you pick up on any psychic visions or whatnot, let me know afterwards."

Peggy set off at a determined walk towards Travis. As I got closer, I got a better view of him. If my grandma were still alive, she would say he looked as if he needed a good wash. His hair was greasy and slicked back from his plump face. He was wearing a T-shirt with the Nithercott logo on it. I noticed it was coming apart at the shoulder seams. His trousers had stains on them which I didn't want to examine too closely.

Peggy plonked herself down on the chair opposite Travis and gave him a wide smile. Travis blinked in surprise and pulled his pint glass closer to him. I noticed it was half full and there was already an empty pint glass on the table.

Peggy said brightly, "Are you Travis? Do you work at that bread factory? I'm Peggy, and this is Karis." She indicated for me to sit down. I sat at her side and gave the confused Travis a small smile.

Travis shot Peggy a defensive look and said, "What's it got to do with you who I am? I don't know why you're bothering me. There are other tables to sit at. Can't a man sit alone and enjoy his pint at the end of a working day?"

"Of course you can, lad," Peggy said, still smiling. "Are you Travis or not?"

He gave her a sharp nod and took a swig from his beer.

Peggy continued, "Then I've got the right person. I know you deliver bread to the corner shop on Alfred Street. I want to know what's happened to it? I've been buying my bread there for years and years and what happened when I went there last week? I'll tell you what happened, Travis. I ended up with something that tasted nothing like the bread I know and love. What happened to it? Did I get a dodgy batch?"

Travis shook his head. He pushed his glass to one side and rested his hands on the table as if settling in for a talk. "It's the new stuff Mr Nithercott has authorised. You're not the only one to complain about it. I can't stand the stuff myself. I don't know what was wrong with the old one. Everyone loved the old one. I've told Mr Nithercott that over and over again, but will he listen? No, he won't. I'm just a delivery driver and what do I know, eh?"

Peggy cast him a sympathetic smile. "I would have thought you would know exactly what the customers wanted. With you being on the front line, so to speak. Mr Nithercott should know that. He should respect your opinion."

Travis lifted his chin slightly. "Yeah, that's right. I am on the front line. I'm not stuck in some office wearing an expensive suit. Mr Nithercott should listen to me. I know what people want. I'm an expert in these matters."

"I'm sure you are," Peggy said. "How long have you worked at the bread factory?"

"About fifteen years now."

Peggy probed, "Have you always been a delivery driver?"

Travis lifted his chin a little more and said proudly, "No, I started off sweeping up on the factory floor. I worked my way up to be a delivery driver. And that's good enough for me. I know my place. Not like some."

"Oh? What do you mean by that?" Peggy asked.

A bitter look came into Travis' eyes. "Let's just say that some people who work at the factory have ideas above their station. They think they're better than anyone else. They think they can make things better when there's nothing wrong with things to begin with." He moved his head a bit closer. "That new bread you got last week, I know the person who's behind that. She was one of those ambitious sorts who never knows when to stop. She used her good looks on old Mr Nithercott to make sure he used a new recipe. What's that word? Beguiled. That's it. She beguiled him with her womanly ways. And now I've been left to sort out the aftermath of her mistake. People don't like new things. They like the old stuff. I can't be doing with too much ambition in a person. It's not right. Anyway, she's gone now."

Peggy suddenly gasped and a hand flew to her chest. "I've just remembered something! One of my friends told me about someone dying at the bread factory. It hasn't been on the news, so I told my friend she must be wrong. Is it true? Has somebody died at the factory?"

Travis gave her a knowing nod. "It's not public knowledge yet, but that ambitious woman I was telling you about just now, it was her. I found her. She was called Carmel."

Peggy leaned forward, her eyes wide. "You found her? How awful for you. You poor thing. If you don't mind me asking, what did you see and where did you find her?"

"I found her at the bottom of some stairs near the offices and the staffroom. It was quite a shock, I can tell you. I'd been in the staffroom having my toast and tea and when I came out, I walked along the corridor outside. As soon as I got to the top of the stairs, I could see Carmel at the bottom. Her legs were at a funny angle so I knew something was wrong." He stopped talking and swallowed. I was surprised to see his eyes shining with tears. He continued, "I thought she'd just fallen at first. But she hadn't. I can't believe she's gone. She was annoying, but she did smile a lot. Even at me."

Peggy shook her head and said, "What a waste of a life. How did she fall? Did you hear her scream or yell?"

Travis shook his head.

"I have my music on when I'm in the staffroom. I don't like talking to other people in there. They talk nonsense and it gets on my nerves. I still had my earphones in when I came out of the room. If Carmel screamed, I didn't hear her."

Peggy tutted. "You poor lad. Did you notice anyone else hanging around the stairs?"

"No, it was just me." He blinked rapidly and swiftly got to his feet. "I have to go. I've got things to do." He abruptly walked away.

Peggy turned to me and said, "He didn't even finish his pint. Was it something I said?"

I said, "He was in love with Carmel. Despite what he said about her, I could clearly feel the love he had for her, and still has. Did you notice that he said Carmel used to smile at him? I think she might have been the only one to do that. Perhaps he was using that petition to get her attention."

Peggy nodded. "I got the impression he was fond of her too. But that puts us in a quandary, doesn't it? What if Travis met Carmel at the top of the stairs and decided to ask her out? What if she laughed in his face, and in a rage, he pushed her down the steps?"

I sighed. "We're no closer to finding out who pushed Carmel."

Peggy downed her gin and tonic in one, smacked her lips together and said, "Let's not give up so easily. You just need to use your psychic powers a bit more. We'll get to the bottom of this. You'll see."

Chapter 15

I drove us back to Peggy's house. On the way, she said, "Are you going to do something about your mum's garden now? No, I suppose you won't, not at this time of the day. It's getting a bit dark, isn't it? You could make a start on the inside. What about giving those windows a quick going-over? I could help you with that if you like? Perhaps a quick blitz in the living room too. I know where Lorena keeps her dusters. No one is living in the house, but the dust still settles. I don't know where it comes from, I just don't."

I pulled up outside Peggy's house, checked the time and said, "I should be getting home. I've got a lot of legal papers to go through and I want to get them sorted out as quick as possible."

Peggy nodded vigorously. "Of course you do. You've got other things to do. Your mum's house can wait a bit longer. You're a busy woman. You get yourself home and sort yourself out." She released her seat belt, grabbed her handbag and gave me a big smile. "It's been smashing to see you again, Karis. Keep in touch, won't you? Let me know how this murder thing goes with Carmel. And if you find out what's wrong with Erin, will you let me know, please? I do worry about you both."

"Yes, of course, I will. Do you want me to walk you to your door?"

Peggy let out a little chuckle. "No, I can find it on my own. You take care now, Karis. Bye for now." She hesitated a few more seconds before getting out of the car.

She gave me three goodbye waves as she walked up the garden path and towards her front door. As she went inside she gave me another wave before closing the front door.

I was about to drive away when a funny feeling came over me. I was getting another vision. I took my hands off the steering wheel and closed my eyes. Was it going to be something involving Carmel again?

It wasn't about Carmel this time. It was about Peggy. I saw her sitting in her living room and talking to a photograph of her late husband. She said, "Jeff, why did you have to leave me so soon? I feel lost without you. I don't know what to do with myself. I try to keep busy, but it's not the same without you. I do miss you."

She sighed heavily, placed a kiss on the frame and then put the photograph back down on the table next to her. She said, "I'll catch up on my telly programmes. I've got plenty to watch. I've been learning such a lot from those documentaries. You would have loved them, Jeff."

My vision progressed and I saw Peggy turning to the television, switching it on and I saw a long list of recorded programmes on the screen. Then, like a photograph album which was being flicked through, I saw Peggy sitting in the same chair watching her TV but wearing different outfits each time. It was like I was fast-forwarding through the next few years of her life, or was I seeing something from the past? Either way, it was obvious Peggy was a lonely woman. I could understand loneliness.

I quickly reversed my car into Mum's driveway and then marched round to Peggy's house. I rapped on the door and when she answered I noticed she was carrying the framed photo of Jeff.

Peggy said, "What is it? Has something happened?"

I said to her, "I can't face going back to an empty house. I'd prefer to stay at Mum's house. Peggy, will you come into Mum's house with me? I haven't been inside since she went into the care home, and I'm worried I'm going to be overcome with memories. I could do with a friend at my side."

"I don't want to intrude on your private time. I'm sure you'd rather be alone, wouldn't you?"

I shook my head. "I don't want to be alone at all. You could help me with a bit of housework. Your house is immaculate and I'd love to get Mum's looking something like that. You'd be doing me a great favour by helping me. We could also have a good gossip about what's been going on in your life. I haven't been in touch with you like I should have. We could make an evening of it. I'll even get us a takeaway."

"A takeaway? On a Tuesday? Karis Booth, you've gone mad." Peggy gave me a smile. "If you really want my company?"

"I do. If that's alright with you?"

Peggy gave me a nod. "I'll pop Jeff back on the table. Come in a minute."

I followed Peggy into her living room and noticed a neat pile of boxes next to one of her chairs. I pointed to them and said, "What's going on here? Have you started a postal delivery service?"

She chuckled. "No, those are my craft supplies. I've been learning all sorts of new crafts on that YouTube. Things I've wanted to know how to do for years but I've never got around to it. I've always enjoyed knitting, but I never got the hang of crocheting. I followed this lovely girl on YouTube who showed me how to do it. I'm going to have a go at cross-stitch too. And jewellery making. And quilting. Those videos are ever so helpful. I like to keep myself busy on a night. You can have a look at some of the craft kits I've ordered. I'll show you what to do. I'm becoming quite an expert at all sorts of things."

Peggy collected her handbag and locked the house up. We completed the short walk to Mum's house and I braced myself for the flood of memories. The memories came, but they were all happy ones. As I walked around the house with Peggy at my side, I told her what I was experiencing. The birthday parties. Christmas mornings. Easter egg hunts around the house and garden. Peggy and Jeff were in most of my memories, and at her insistence, I described what she was wearing and what Jeff was saying. We shed more than a few happy tears as we completed our tour of the house.

"Well," I declared, "that was very therapeutic. It's made me very hungry. What kind of takeaway would you like? Pizza? Chinese? Indian? Thai?"

Peggy replied, "That's too much choice! Can we just go for a pizza, please? Can we have some of that garlic bread too? I do love it. I know it makes me stink to high heaven the following day, but I can't get enough of it."

I placed our order and then had a good look in Mum's kitchen and discovered a couple of bottles of wine. I held them up to Peggy and said, "Shall we?"

Peggy grinned. "One bottle for you, and one for me? Stick a straw in the end and we're good to go." She laughed when she caught my startled expression. "Only kidding. One glass will be enough for me. Perhaps two. At a push, three."

Before I opened the wine, Peggy insisted on having a quick dust around in the living room. While she did that, I phoned Erin. She didn't answer, so I left a message for her.

Twenty minutes later, Peggy and I were settled in the living room with glasses of wine at our sides and pizza on our laps.

I found a box set of murder mysteries and said to Peggy, "Perhaps we should watch something like this and get our little grey cells working."

"Excellent idea, Sherlock. Or should I say, Miss Marple? Hang on, should I be Miss Marple and you can be Hercule Poirot? What about that Jessica Fletcher from Murder, She Wrote? If we're going to be investigating a murder, we really should decide who we're going to be." She reached for a big slice of garlic bread.

"I think we should just be ourselves. We're good enough as we are."

With her cheeks bulging with garlic bread, Peggy nodded and said, "I always knew I was perfect and now you've confirmed it. My Jeff said I was perfect in every way. The silly old fool." She smiled at the memory.

We both managed to get on to our third glass of wine by the time the murder mystery had ended. We were feeling pleasantly smug with ourselves as we'd both worked out who the murderer was before the sleuth did.

I said to Peggy, "I'm having a lovely time. Thanks for being with me."

Peggy was just about to reply when a thunderous knock sounded out on the front door.

Peggy exclaimed, "Who the heck is calling at this time of the night? Karis, it's the murderer! They've found out we're looking into Carmel's death! They've tracked us down! Quick, find a weapon." She grabbed the nearest empty pizza box and got to her feet.

Luckily, I had a now-empty wine bottle at my side, so I grabbed that and slowly followed Peggy to the front door. In my slightly drunken state, I was convinced that Carmel's murderer was standing there too.

I raised my empty bottle and quickly pulled back the front door.

Peggy rushed forward and bashed the man standing there with her empty pizza box. She declared, "You don't scare us! We know what you did and we will seek justice! Take that!"

DCI Parker warded off the pizza box attack and cried out, "Whoa! Stop that immediately! It's against the law to attack a police officer. Peggy, you nearly had my eye out with the corner of that box then."

Peggy lowered her box, and I lowered the wine bottle.

"Well, well, well," Peggy said. "It's the London boy. Have you solved Carmel's murder yet? No? I didn't think you had. Karis and me have been making excellent progress on the case, and we'll have the murderer locked up before the end of tomorrow."

His expression hardened. "I only came here to check on your mum's house, Karis. Mum told me no one is living here, so I was suspicious when I saw the lights on. What's this about your murder investigation?" His nose wrinkled. "Have you been eating garlic? Are you both drunk?"

"Yes, we are!" Peggy declared happily. She reached out, grabbed the detective chief inspector's sleeve and pulled him into the house. "We'd better talk about this murder investigation right away," she said. "You're making a pig's ear out of it. Thinking it was an accident? Pah! Let us put you right."

Chapter 16

Peggy dragged DCI Parker into the living room and pushed him onto the sofa. She sat at his side, patted his knee and said, "Would you like a drink of wine? We can spare you a glass."

He said rather testily, "No, thanks. I think there's been enough drinking going on in here."

"Please yourself," Peggy said as she reached for her half-full glass. She took a sip, smacked her lips together in appreciation and put her glass back down. "Now then, Seb, let's have a bit of a chat before we get down to business."

"It's DCI Parker," came his curt reply.

Peggy patted his knee again playfully and said, "Not at this time of the night, lad. You're not on duty, are you?"

He shook his head.

"Well then," Peggy declared, "you are going to be Seb to us tonight. If you don't like it, you can leave."

"You can call me Seb for now," he relented.

"Right then, Seb, tell us what you've been up to. I know you went down to London and picked up some funny ways, but what brought you back to Leeds? Have you come back to keep an eye on your mum and dad? Or did you come back for a promotion? I heard from your mum you were a detective inspector down in London, but now you're a detective chief inspector. Does that mean you moved back here for a promotion? Or was it to return to your roots? Or to look after your mum and dad? Or maybe it was a mixture of all?"

Her questions were making me feel dizzy and I couldn't remember her first one.

Seb looked like a rabbit caught in the headlights, and for a moment I was tempted to ask Peggy to stop her interrogation. But I wanted to know why he'd come back too, so I cradled my glass of wine, settled back in the chair and watched the show unfold.

With my defences down, I noticed Seb looked quite handsome in his casual wear of jeans and a dark jumper. Hmm. He'd been working out too. The sober side of my mind tried to tell me to stop having such observations, but I ignored it.

Seb began, "As usual, Peggy, you're right about all of those reasons. I did get the promotion based on me returning to Leeds. Not that I minded as I have missed this place. And you're right about me wanting to keep an eye on Mum and Dad. They've both had health issues, and I want to be around in case they need me."

Peggy gave him a nod. "Yes, I know about their health issues. They're only at the end of the street, after all. We all stick together around here, and you can rest assured that if anything happened to them, we'd look after them."

He flashed her a brief smile. "I know you would, but I still want to be near. I've just been over to their house now which is why I noticed the lights on in Lorena's house." He looked my way and added, "I wasn't expecting to find you here. I thought you'd be back at your own house having a dip in one of your swimming pools."

I frowned at him. Was there a hint of amusement in his voice? Was he making fun of my lovely swimming pools? The cheek of him.

Peggy tapped him on the shoulder and he turned his head back to her. She said, "How far have you got with your investigation? Karis told me what you said to her earlier about her visions. That's very rude of you, Seb. You know her visions are real. Or at least, you used to." Her face creased in concern. "Now that I come to think of it, I never did find out why you two fell out when you were young. Why was it? You were such good friends. You did everything together. It all changed when you went to high school. Seb, it was probably your fault. What did you do to upset Karis so much?"

Seb pulled at the neck of his jumper and said, "It's all in the past. I don't want to talk about it."

The wine had given me a strength which I didn't know I had. I'd already shouted at my soon-to-be ex-husband today, so I reasoned another shouting match wouldn't go amiss.

I aimed my wine glass in Seb's direction and said loudly, "I'll tell you why, Peggy. Oh yes, I'll tell you why."

Seb shot me a pleading look. "There's no need to go over the past, Karis."

Peggy said, "Let her get it out. She's having a good day for releasing her past emotions and it's not your place to tell her to stop doing so. Don't be so selfish, Sebastian Parker, think about Karis. She's obviously carrying a great hurt from her past which you're at the centre of. Let her vent. Be a man about it."

Seb gave me a resigned look and said, "Go on then, you might as well tell me how you feel."

I took a fortifying drink of wine, set my glass down and shuffled to the end of my seat. "Peggy, you're right about us being best friends in our youth. I thought we always would be. Seb knew about my psychic abilities right from when we were little. He loved it when I experienced something and he encouraged me to do it more and more. I told him about my visions before I even told Mum or Dad. He believed me every time when I told him about an image I'd seen in my head."

Seb looked down at his knees and didn't say a word.

I was getting into the flow now. "Things changed when we went to high school. I made the mistake of telling my school friends about some of my visions. I thought they'd be as understanding as Seb. I was mistaken. They made fun of me and started to call me Krazy Karis. Yes, crazy with a K. They even scrolled it across my books and on my desk. There were nasty things written about me in the girls' bathroom. I confided in Seb and he was so supportive. At first. But then things changed. One day I overheard him laughing and joking with some people, and he called me Krazy Karis too."

I stopped talking as those hurtful memories whooshed into my brain and exploded like a firework. Every insult, every jeer, every smirk from my school days came back to me one after the other. My voice was thick with emotion but I carried on, "I asked Seb why he would say such things, and he said it was time I grew out of my visions, and they were making me look like an idiot. He refused to talk to me after that. We were a couple at that stage, but he just left my life like I meant nothing to him."

Peggy let out a loud gasp of outrage. She turned her full force on Seb and shouted, "How could you? How could you do that to Karis? Everyone on this street knows about her special gift, and we all support her. Even your mum and dad support her! What sort of a man are you? You lily-livered coward! You namby-pamby, yellow-belly excuse of a man!"

Seb gave her a slow nod. "I admit it. I was a coward. I wasn't strong enough to stand up for Karis. She was much stronger than me and gave people a mouthful when they made fun of her. But I gave in to peer pressure. I wanted to fit in with the majority rather than be with someone who others were making fun of. I was weak. I'm so ashamed of my behaviour." He looked at me and said, "I did come round here and tried to apologise to you. But Erin answered the door and insulted me every time. She even threw a bucket of water over me once. She said I didn't deserve to be on the same planet as you. I agreed with her. No apology would ever make up for how I treated you."

I gave him a small smile. "I didn't know about you coming round here to apologise."

He gave me a smile in return. "I don't expect you to forgive me. I can't even forgive myself."

I thought about how I felt over Robbie's shooting and said, "I can sympathise with that feeling."

Peggy said, "Seb, you should have made more of an effort to apologise. Well, we can't change the past, but you can make amends for it now. When Karis told you about her vision concerning Carmel, why didn't you believe her?"

"Because I'm a level-headed police officer who's been trained to deal with facts only. Truth be told, I did believe her. But I could hardly admit to that, could I? I'm too stubborn to do so. One of my many faults, so I've been told. Can we talk about something else now? Talking about how I treated Karis makes me feel worse than any criminal I've dealt with. Peggy, I want to know what you meant by your earlier comments. What's this about your murder investigation? Karis, Have you picked up on anything else concerning Carmel? Have you had any more visions or feelings? You can tell me about them."

He gave me a big smile and he looked very much like the friend from my youth. However, those memories from high school were still fresh in my mind, and I was wary of how he would take the information I was about to give him. No matter how much he smiled at me, he wasn't going to get back in my good books that quickly. However, I did want Carmel's murderer to be found, so I put my feelings to one side.

Between Peggy and myself, we told Seb what we'd found out about Carmel and her relationship with Travis.

Seb listened quietly and then said, "I've already questioned Travis about his whereabouts at the time of the incident. There's a CCTV camera along the corridor leading to the staffroom. It points at the door, and the footage shows Travis walking along with his earphones in."

"CCTV?" I said. "Why didn't you tell us about this earlier? Have you checked the footage that looks over the stairs?"

He shook his head. "For some reason, the camera doesn't cover the stairs. You were right about Carmel being pregnant, though. She was in the early stages of her pregnancy."

Peggy shook her head. "The poor girl. What are you going to do next, Seb? How can we help you?"

He replied, "You can help me by staying out of this investigation. If Karis is right, it means there's a murderer out there. I don't want either of you putting yourselves in danger." He hesitated and then added, "But thank you for letting me know what you've found out. This could be very useful. I'll let myself out." He got to his feet and looked down at me. "I know this is long overdue, Karis, but I truly am sorry for how I acted during my foolish youth. I have no excuses."

I gave him a half shrug. I would have loved to say I'd forgiven him, but I wasn't at that stage yet.

As soon as he'd left the house, Peggy rubbed her hands together and said eagerly, "Let's see who can solve this murder investigation first — us or the London boy." She yawned and looked at the clock. "Is that the time? Karis Booth, you're a bad influence on me. I never stay up so late. I'd better get myself back into my own house and into bed before the neighbours start talking."

She stood up, finished the rest of her wine and walked unsteadily towards the front door.

I helped her out of the house, along the path and into her house. Because I was more steady on my feet than Peggy, I helped her upstairs and into her nightwear. She hummed and sang to herself as I did so. It was like looking after a child. I tucked her into bed, gave her a kiss goodnight on the forehead and then left her house making sure the door was locked.

Five minutes later, I settled down in my childhood bed and smiled at the posters which Mum had kept on the wall. Having had three glasses of wine, I expected to fall asleep straight away. But that didn't happen. Something was niggling at the back of my brain. Somebody had said something today which was bothering me. I couldn't quite put my finger on what it was, but still, the feeling persisted.

I eventually drifted off to sleep and had dreams which involved Peggy and me racing after faceless murderers.

As soon as I woke up, I knew what had been bothering me the night before.

Chapter 17

"I can't believe how stupid I've been!" Peggy exclaimed.

I was in Peggy's kitchen the following morning, and she looked surprisingly bright and awake considering she'd had a late night and three glasses of wine.

I said, "It came to me this morning. I knew something was bothering me at the back of my mind last night, but I couldn't work out what it was. As soon as I woke up, it became clear. Both Travis and Cyril referred to Mr Nithercott as old Mr Nithercott which made me wonder if there was a young Mr Nithercott." I took a drink of the tea that Peggy had insisted on making me. It was extra strong and gave me the caffeine boost that I needed this morning.

Peggy said, "I heard Travis say that too, but it didn't register with me at the time either. Of course, there's a young Mr Nithercott too. I knew that." She shook her head at herself. "I don't know why I didn't point this out to you. I must be getting old or something. We haven't taken young Mr Nithercott into account in our investigation. I must admit that I don't know much about him. I don't even know his first name."

I said, "I've been online this morning to find out more about him. He's called Flynn, and he's worked in the family business for years. He's Mr Nithercott's grandson. Flynn's father died a few years ago."

Peggy nodded. "I think I remember something in the papers about that. How old is he?"

"He's thirty-three. He's single, and from the photographs I've seen online, he's quite handsome but in a way that's too obvious, if you know what I mean?

Everything about him is perfect and he doesn't have any physical flaws."

Peggy's eyes narrowed. "Never trust a man who is too handsome. Do you think he's the father of Carmel's baby?"

"I don't know. We should talk to him, but I can't think of a reason as to why we should. We can't just turn up at the factory for a chat. I suppose DCI Parker has spoken to him about Carmel's death."

Peggy shook her head in disgust. "Don't refer to Seb by his official title. He doesn't deserve it. I still can't get over what he did to you at school."

I gave her a shrug in the hope of convincing her I wasn't bothered.

My phone rang at that point. I looked at it but I didn't recognise the number. I answered it and listened to the woman on the other end. Once she'd given me her message, I said I'd be there right away.

I ended the call and said to Peggy, "That was a nurse from the hospital."

"Who's dead now?"

"No one. But Cyril Simpson has been injured. He's broken his leg. He had my number and insisted the nurse phone me this morning. He wants to talk to me."

Peggy's eyebrows rose. "Cyril? Cyril from the care home? You barely know each other. Why does he want to talk to you?"

"I don't know, but that's what I'm going to find out. Do you want to come with me?"

Peggy took a long drink of her tea, put the cup down and said, "Of course I do! It could be something to do with our murder investigation. Let me pop to the toilet before we set off. That tea always goes straight through me."

Cyril looked very pale when we saw him in his hospital bed later. His right leg was in plaster and had been raised above the bedcovers. The nurse told us he'd been in an agitated state since they brought him in yesterday and kept calling my name. They'd had to sedate him to enable him to have a good night's sleep. As soon as he'd woken up, Cyril had badgered the nurse to get in touch with me. I was as confused as Peggy as to why he should want to talk to me.

Peggy sat on a chair at one side of Cyril's bed. and I sat at the other.

Cyril gave me a tired smile and said, "Thank you for coming to see me. You were so kind to me yesterday, and I didn't know who else to call. I had a feeling you'd appreciate what I'm about to tell you. It's funny how we were talking about Nithercott bread yesterday, and now here I am as a result of that company."

I felt my stomach clench in apprehension. "What do you mean by that? What happened yesterday?"

Cyril indicated his head towards his broken leg. "That's what happened to me yesterday. The doctor said I'm lucky to be alive. He said I could have broken my neck in that fall down the stairs."

Peggy spoke up, "Fall down the stairs? What do you mean by that? Come on, Cyril, get on with your tale."

Cyril gave her an impatient look. "That's what I'm trying to do, Peggy, if you give me a minute."

I was concerned about how pale Cyril's face was and said, "You take your time. We're not in any rush."

"After our conversation yesterday, Karis, you got me thinking about that new Nithercott bread again. I thought if old Mr Nithercott didn't want to listen to me, then young Mr Nithercott might. I went to see him after I left the care home. I went into his office and politely explained my predicament. I told him all about Maggie and what the bread meant to us." He pressed his lips together and took a moment to compose himself. "It was a mistake to go there. Young Mr Nithercott barely listened to what I was saying. He kept tapping away on his phone and when he did look at me, it was like I was a nuisance."

Peggy tutted in disgust.

Cyril carried on, "He didn't even care when I said Maggie was in a care home and the memory of Nithercott bread was the only thing that brought a spark to her eyes. When I'd finished talking, he said he couldn't care less about the old bread and it was people like me who were causing delays in his plans. He said he had a ten-year plan and he was sick to death of people interfering in that. He went on to say it was one obstacle after another. He muttered about having just got rid of one obstacle, and he was prepared to do it again."

Peggy interrupted him, "What did he mean by obstacles? Did you ask him?"

Cyril said, "I didn't. He just went ranting on and on, and he started shouting at me. I told Karis yesterday that I don't like people shouting, and I made to leave the office. That young Mr Nithercott was very rude and he swore at me and told me to get out of the factory and never return. I went as quick as my legs would carry me out of the office and along the corridor. I was halfway down the stairs when I could have sworn I felt someone push me. I toppled all the way down and I must've banged my head or something because everything went black. When I came round, young Mr Nithercott was kneeling next to me. He told me I'd slipped and fallen down the stairs by accident. He said he'd called an ambulance and they would be here soon."

I shared a shocked look with Peggy and then said to Cyril, "Do you think young Mr Nithercott pushed you down the stairs?"

Cyril gave me a slow nod. "I think that's exactly what happened. He was in a foul mood when I left his office. He had a look in his eyes as if he'd lost control of his senses. He tried to convince me it was an accident, but I definitely felt hands on my back before I fell. I can't tell the police as they wouldn't believe me. They'd believe Mr Nithercott, wouldn't they?" He looked towards his elevated leg. "I could have died. Who would visit Maggie then?"

Peggy had a face like thunder. She said to Cyril, "We've got contacts in the police force. We'll get in touch with them. Then we'll go and see that nasty Mr Nithercott."

Cyril said, "I don't want to cause any trouble."

I reached over and gently patted his pale hand. I said, "You're not the one who's going to cause trouble; it's going to be me. I'll contact the police. I'll tell them everything. You get as much rest as you can, Cyril. After I've spoken to the police, I'll go and sit with Maggie. I was going to see Mum later anyway."

Peggy piped up, "I'll sit with her too. I'll get some of my friends to do the same."

Tears flooded Cyril's old eyes. He gave me a gentle smile and said, "I don't know how you managed to come into my life yesterday, Karis, but I'm so glad you did. Will you really contact the police about this?"

I gave him a firm nod. "I'm going to speak to Mr Nithercott too. He doesn't scare me."

Cyril shot me a warning glance. "Be careful around Mr Nithercott. He's a bad one. I felt that as soon as I entered his office. Be very careful around him."

Chapter 18

When we left the hospital I said to Peggy, "I'm going to the police station now. I'm going to tell Robbie about this latest incident. He'll take care of everything."

Peggy gave me a pained look. "As much as I want to see Flynn Nithercott brought to justice for Cyril's accident, I've got some commitments this morning, and I can't come with you."

"What commitments?"

"I've got some old friends who are housebound. I call on them on a regular basis and do things for them around the house. I don't like to let them down as I'm often the only company they have all week. Would you mind going to the police station without me? You can let me know how you get on later."

"Where do these friends of yours live?"

"Joyce lives twenty minutes away and there'll be a bus soon. If I speed up, I can make it to the bus stop in time."

"Peggy, I can give you a lift there. You don't need to worry about getting the bus. I'm happy to give you a lift."

Peggy shook her head. "But you need to get to the police station as soon as possible."

"I insist on giving you a lift first. Don't argue."

I dropped Peggy off at her friend's house and then headed over to the police station. I asked for Robbie at the reception area and he came out to see me.

My first question to him was, "How's Erin? I left a message for her on the phone last night, but she hasn't got back to me. I've tried her again this morning and she's still not answering. Is everything alright with her?"

Robbie gave me one of his kind smiles and said, "She is absolutely fine. She's back at work this morning after having a good night's sleep. Now then, have you come here to check up on Erin or is there something else you want to talk to me about? I understand from my new friend, Sebastian Parker, that you've been interfering in his investigation. I told him he must have the wrong Karis Booth as the one I know would never do anything like that." He gave me a little chuckle and took me over to the side of the reception area.

I quickly told him about my visit to Cyril at the hospital. All joviality left Robbie's face.

He said, "This is a serious turn of events. It doesn't put Flynn Nithercott in a good light. I can't do anything with this information as I'm not dealing with the case. You'll have to speak to Seb about it immediately. Come on, I'll take you over to his office."

"Can't you tell him for me? He'll only think I'm interfering again."

"But you are interfering again. However, Cyril got in contact with you and volunteered this information. You did the right thing by coming here and letting us know. At least you weren't reckless enough to go zooming around to Flynn Nithercott's office to confront him face-to-face. That would have been a silly thing to do." He gave me a long look and continued, "You were going to go over there and confront him, weren't you? I can see it on your face."

I looked away from his accusing eyes and said, "I did consider it for a minute. Perhaps two minutes. But like a good citizen, I came here instead."

I followed Robbie through a set of doors and he pointed me in the direction of Seb's office. As I walked over there, I noticed there was a younger man in the office with Seb and the door was ajar. I couldn't help but overhear their conversation.

The younger man said, "Seeing as you grew up around here, you'll know your way around town. I was in the year below you at school. You won't remember me, but I remember you. You used to hang around with that weird girl." He clicked his fingers in the air. "She had a nickname. What was it now?"

Seb had his back to me and didn't see me standing at the door. He said, "Krazy Karis. That was her nickname."

The other man burst out laughing and said, "That's it! Krazy Karis. Didn't she think she was a psychic and could see into the future? What a freak!"

I took a sharp intake of breath. Seb turned his head and looked my way. Panic filled his face and he shot to his feet.

I turned around and walked quickly away, my eyes stinging. Hearing that awful nickname said with such derision brought a host of unwelcome memories crashing down on me.

I was outside and heading towards my car when I felt a hand on my shoulder. I turned around to find Seb standing there.

He held his hands out and said, "Karis, I'm so sorry about that. I wasn't making fun of you. Honest. I realise it didn't look that way to you. I keep putting my foot in it, don't I?"

I tried to smile, but my mouth refused to cooperate. I said tightly, "You were only answering a question. It's not your fault."

Seb ran a hand through his hair. "I shouldn't have told him the name. I should have said I didn't remember it. I'm a prize idiot. If I find out he uses that stupid nickname anywhere in my vicinity, I'll arrest him. I'll lock him away and put some gaffer tape over his mouth so he can never speak again. The same goes for anyone else who uses it."

I managed a small smile. "And what would you arrest people for exactly?"

"I don't know, I'd think of something. Karis, what are you doing here?"

"Before I tell you that, let me make it clear that I didn't go out seeking this new information. Cyril phoned me."

"Cyril? Who are you talking about?"

I quickly told him about Cyril and his so-called accident.

Seb's nostrils flared and he said, "This puts a different slant on the whole Carmel incident. I didn't know about Cyril's accident. I should have been told about it immediately. Accident or not, anything involving the Nithercott factory needs to be reported to me." He put his hands on my shoulders, looked me directly in the eyes and said, "I've no right to ask you this, not after what you've just overheard, but I'd like you to come with me to the factory when I confront Flynn Nithercott."

"Why?"

"Because I want to know if you experience anything while I'm interviewing him. Any psychic visions or premonitions. Any emotions you get from him. You were always good with this when we were little. You were great at working out when my mum was in the perfect mood for me to ask her for ice cream. Do you remember that?" He gave me a gentle smile. "Since we spoke last night, I've done nothing but recall all the good times we had together. You were such a good friend to me, and I was the worst friend in the world to you." He took his hands off my shoulders.

"Yes, you were the worst friend in the world. Possibly the universe. But I will come with you to speak to Flynn Nithercott. I'm sure he'll like to know how Cyril is getting on following his accident at the factory."

"Good," Seb said. "We'll go in my car."

He made to walk away.

I put my hands on my hips. "Don't you give me orders, Detective Chief Inspector Parker. I'm capable of driving to the factory on my own. And that's what I'm going to do."

Seb said, "Stop being so stubborn. I'm only offering you a lift."

"I'll meet you there," I said stubbornly.

I didn't give him another look as I got into my car and drove away. It gave me a small amount of pleasure to see Seb's confused look in my rear-view mirror. Serves him right. Trying to give me orders! The nerve of him. A couple of apologies doesn't make us best friends again.

Chapter 19

I took an instant dislike to Flynn Nithercott. It wasn't just because he'd pushed Cyril down the stairs: there was something inherently nasty about him. I could feel it the second we entered his office.

His office was located in between old Mr Nithercott's office and the staffroom. As we walked up the stairs towards his office, Seb told me the CCTV camera hadn't been aimed at Flynn's door on the day of Carmel's accident. That was convenient, I thought to myself.

Flynn Nithercott invited us to sit down. There was an impatient tone in his voice and a hardness in his eyes. He sat on the leather chair behind his desk, clasped his hands together and rested them on the desk. I noticed his knuckles were white. He looked like a wild animal who was getting ready to attack.

Flynn said, "What can I help you with, Detective Chief Inspector? I thought you had all the information you needed about Carmel's accident."

Seb hadn't introduced me when we'd entered, and Flynn didn't ask who I was. He'd given me a dismissive glance and then acted as if I wasn't there.

Seb began, "We're still making enquiries about Carmel Johnson's death."

"Why?" Flynn snapped. "It was an accident."

"That's for us to decide," Seb continued. "Mr Nithercott, how well did you know Carmel Johnson?"

A muscle twitched in Flynn's jaw. "What do you mean by that?"

"How was she as an employee?"

"She was okay. Reliable. Punctual. Got on well with the other members of staff. Why are you asking me this?"

Seb's tone was polite as he continued, "It's routine. How did you get on with her?"

Flynn glanced at some drawers underneath the desk. It was only a quick glance, but I noticed it.

Flynn said, "I didn't have much to do with her. She spent time with Grandad, though. He liked her for some reason. She bothered him constantly about her new ideas for our bread. He's such a soft touch that he actually put some of her ideas into practice." He gave a half shrug. "Some of the things she came up were decent enough. Sales have increased somewhat." He flashed a glance at the drawer again. "Is there anything else? I've got a lot of work on today."

Seb opened his palm in my direction. "This is Mrs Booth. She was contacted by a friend of hers earlier, Mr Cyril Simpson. Do you know Mr Simpson?"

"No. Should I?"

I had to press my lips tightly together to stop myself shouting at Flynn Nithercott. Seb had warned me to stay quiet throughout the interview and I was finding it a challenge to do so.

Seb said, "Mr Simpson came to see you yesterday. I checked with the young man on reception just now who's confirmed that. Mr Simpson is an elderly man and he spoke to you about your bread. He wasn't happy with the new recipe."

Flynn had the nerve to smirk. "That old fool. Yeah, I remember him now. Turned up and then gave me an earful of his complaints. I can't do with moaning customers. If they don't like our bread, they should stop buying it."

It was taking all my willpower not to say anything.

Seb's tone was now icy cold as he said, "Mr Simpson suffered an accident here yesterday, as you well know. He fell down the stairs. Apparently."

Flynn said, "Apparently? What are you getting at? I don't like the tone in your voice."

"Two similar accidents in a short period of time is more than a coincidence, Mr Nithercott. I've checked the stairs and there's nothing sticking up which would cause a person to trip. The carpet is of the anti-slip material, so that isn't at fault either."

"Now just a minute!" Flynn exploded.

As he did so, a vision came to me. Flynn's cry of outrage faded and I was oblivious to my surroundings as the image became clearer.

Carmel was in here. Her face was red with rage. She flung something at Flynn and stormed out of the office. Flynn picked the item up, opened a drawer at his side and flung the item in. He slammed the drawer shut.

The vision faded.

There was something important in that drawer at Flynn's side. I had to look inside. My vision showed me it wasn't locked, but I could hardly lean over and open it.

Flynn continued to shout at Seb, and Seb continued to remain professional.

Think! Think! What could I do?

My attention went to a jug of water on the table behind Flynn. There were some empty glasses next to the jug. There was an obvious move I could make, but would it work? It was a ridiculous move and Flynn would see right through it. But I had to do something.

Doing an impression of a gentle Victorian lady, I wafted my hand over my face and declared loudly, "My goodness! Isn't it hot in here? I feel all flushed. Would you mind if I had a glass of water?" I wafted my hand even more.

Flynn was too busy shouting at Seb to hear my request.

Nonetheless, I went on, "I am going to pass out with this heat. I need water!"

Seb shot me a worried look. "I'll get it for you."

I was on my feet in a flash. "No need. I'll get it!"

I went over to the jug and poured a full glass of water. My hands were shaking and a fair amount of water splashed onto the carpet. Keeping up my maiden-in-distress act, I moved closer to Flynn and announced, "I feel so weak and feeble. I can't hold on to this heavy glass."

Then, in the most melodramatic fashion, I threw the water over Flynn Nithercott.

He jumped to his feet, turned to me, and let out a very rude curse.

I put the glass down and said, "I'm so sorry! It was an accident. Let me dry you. Have you got any tissues? You must have. Let me look for them."

"Get out! Just get out!" Flynn shouted.

I ignored him, shoved him to one side and opened the desk at his side. There it was. That was what Carmel had thrown at Flynn.

I picked the item up and said, "Oh, this is a baby scan photo. Are you going to be a father, Mr Nithercott? How wonderful."

Flynn made a lunge for the photo, but I nimbly moved to one side and said, "This has got the mother's name on it. Carmel Johnson. I didn't know you were a couple."

There was a stunned silence.

Seb came over to my side and took the photo from me. He treated me to a long look which said, "I'll be talking to you later about your little performance, Mrs Booth."

Flynn held his hands up, "I can explain."

Seb said, "The facts are speaking for themselves. You've lied to me about your relationship with Carmel Johnson. What else have you been lying about, Mr Nithercott?"

A mask of rage came over Flynn's face. "Alright! We did have a fling, but I never wanted to be a father. I told Carmel that. It was her responsibility to make sure that never happened. She stormed in here and told me she was going to have our baby. I couldn't have that! I have a ten-year plan, and it doesn't involve babies. I told her the child was her problem and she should deal with it. She threatened to tell Grandad. I knew he'd force me to take responsibility." He paused and his shoulders dropped. "I didn't mean to kill her. I thought a fall down the steps would get rid of the baby."

I looked away from Flynn's face. I couldn't bear to look at him.

Seb started saying something about arresting Flynn Nithercott. I wasn't paying attention. All I could think about was Carmel and the bright future which had been taken away from her.

Chapter 20

After receiving a dressing-down from Seb, I left the factory and went over to Erin's Café. I found my sister behind the counter. A lone customer sat at a table in the corner.

Erin's face lit up as I entered. "Hey there! I've been trying to call you. Sorry I didn't return your messages from last night and this morning. Have you got time for a cuppa and a slice of chocolate fudge cake? I've made it fresh this morning."

"I'll say yes to both." I pulled a stool out in front of the counter and sat down. Erin came to sit at my side bringing tea and cake for us both.

The lone customer stood up, waved to Erin and left the café. I heard Erin's soft sigh.

I said to her, "What's going on with the café? Why is it so quiet?"

"Never mind about the café. It's just one of those seasonal things. I want to know what's happened this morning. I got through to Peggy and she told me about Cyril and his fall down the stairs. She said you were going to call in at the police station. I phoned Robbie and he told me you left the station with Sebastian Parker." She pulled a look of disgust. "I don't know how you can bear to be anywhere near that treacherous man."

I pulled my tea towards me. "He's not so bad."

Erin pinched my arm. "Who are you? Where's my sister gone? Are you a robot?"

I laughed. "Don't be silly. Did Peggy tell you about our visit last night from Seb?"

Erin shook her head. "No, she didn't." She pulled my slice of cake towards her. "You are not having a bite of this delectable cake until you tell me everything. And I mean everything. Don't leave one single detail out."

I proceeded to tell Erin every little detail. She made the occasional comment in between shovelling cake into her mouth. I was worried she was going to start on my cake soon.

When I'd finished, she shook her head and said, "I can't believe it. How could Flynn Nithercott do that? You hear about these things, but you don't expect them to happen so close to home. Poor Carmel. I don't understand why Flynn Nithercott pushed Cyril down the stairs, though. What had Cyril done to annoy him?"

"I think he was just in the wrong place at the wrong time. Flynn probably pushed him for the fun of it. That Flynn Nithercott is a nasty piece of work. I'm glad he's going to be locked up."

Erin looked at me for a moment before saying, "Are you glad you got involved? Are you glad you solved Carmel's murder?"

I flashed her a swift smile. "I'm glad I acted on my visions. I wouldn't say I solved her murder. I only wish I could have prevented it."

"You didn't know she was going to die. Don't be too hard on yourself. I bet DCI Sebastian Parker is glad you helped him. He wouldn't have got a confession from Flynn if you hadn't opened that drawer. He should be thankful to you."

"I think he was, in a grudgingly roundabout sort of way. He did tell me off, but it was a toned-down telling-off. I think he's truly sorry for what happened at high school. Anyway, I can't dwell on the past. What's done is done."

Erin's eyes narrowed. "I can dwell on the past. And when I see that excuse of a man, I'll tell him how I feel about him." She gave me a nod to confirm her words.

Then she did something which made my heart skip a beat. She rested her hands on her lower abdomen.

I jabbed an accusing figure at her. "You're pregnant!"

Erin smiled. "I am. I'm surprised it's taken you so long to pick up on that. Call yourself a psychic!"

I stared at her stomach which was ever so slightly rounded. I said, "I don't always pick up on things from close family members. Why didn't you tell me straight away?"

Her smile fell. "Robbie and I decided not to say anything until I was further along. Not after the last three times."

"Three times?" I looked into her eyes. "Erin, I know about two miscarriages. When you did you have a third one?"

Tears came to her eyes. "It was after Robbie had been shot. It must have been the shock. Karis, I think it will be different this time. I think this baby will survive. Can you feel anything? Can you look into my future? Please."

I put my hand on her stomach and concentrated. "I'm not picking up on any images. That doesn't mean anything. Like I said, my visions don't always work with close family members. Erin, is this why Robbie has been so protective of you?"

She nodded. "When I lost the third baby two years ago, I couldn't get pregnant again. Robbie used some of our savings so that we could try IVF. We only had enough money for one go. And this is it. I've had to take time off work because of the procedures. I've had to let staff go too because I don't have the money to pay them." She gave me a wobbly smile. "I think I'll have to sell the café. It's not making a profit for me because I can't put in the hours. But the sacrifices will be worth it when I hold my child in my arms."

The café door opened and a couple came in.

Erin stood up and said, "Customers. Great. Will you excuse me while I see to them?"

"Erin, is there anything I can do to help you with your pregnancy or work?"

"No, thank you. Robbie and I will manage. We always do." She walked over to the customers and showed them to a table.

The café around me faded and a vision came to me. It was bright and clear.

Erin was heavily pregnant. She was standing behind the counter and serving a customer. There was pain on her face.

The customer walked away.

Erin clutched her stomach and cried out in pain. Blood trickled down her legs.

The vision changed. I was now looking at a hospital bed.

Erin was in bed, her face as white as the sheets which covered her. Her stomach was smaller now. Robbie was holding her in his arms. They were both crying. There was no baby in sight.

The vision faded. I was back in the café and Erin was walking towards me.

"Karis, what's wrong?" she asked. "Are you crying? Why?"

I gave her the biggest smile I could manage. "These are happy tears. Listen, I've got to go. I've got those divorce papers to sort out. I'll call you later. Take good care of yourself. Why don't you close the café when those customers have gone? You could go home and get into bed. You have to take things easy."

She shook her head. "You're as bad as Robbie. I couldn't possibly stay in bed. I need to be doing something."

I gave her a hug before leaving the café. I knew my vision was an image of what could happen based on the present circumstances. I also knew that if the present circumstances were changed, then the future could change too.

I had an idea of what I could do. Well, more than one idea. There was no way I was going to let Erin and Robbie lose this baby. I would do everything I could to help them.

Chapter 21

It was two days later when I was ready to reveal my plan to Erin and Robbie. I was sitting in their living room with Peggy at my side. I had revealed everything to Peggy including my vision of Erin losing her baby. Peggy had agreed with my plans and had thrown herself into action with a surprising amount of energy.

Erin and Robbie were sitting on the sofa and holding hands. Peggy and I were in armchairs at their side.

Erin looked at me, over at Peggy and then back at me. She said, "You both look as if you're going to burst with some news. Either that or you're constipated. Don't keep us waiting any longer. Karis, you said you had something important to tell us. Come on; out with it."

I began. "I'm going to sell my house and move into Mum's. I've already put my house on the market."

"Really?" Erin asked. "Why have you done that? I thought you liked your house. If I had a house with two swimming pools, I'd never leave it."

Robbie pulled on Erin's hand and said, "I think we'll find out Karis' big plans quicker if you keep quiet. Save your questions for the end."

"Thanks, Robbie," I said. "I'm going to move into Mum's house because I love living there. The neighbours are wonderful."

"That's me," Peggy said cheerfully.

I smiled at her. "The other neighbours are okay too. There are too many awful memories associated with my house. I want a fresh start. The divorce is going through now. Gavin has put aside any claims to those investments. I think that was on the advice of his solicitor. Anyway, with one thing and another, I've got more money than I know what to do with." I shared a smile with Peggy. "That's not strictly true. I know what I am going to do with it. Erin, I'd like to invest in your café. The building next door is up for sale and I think the café should be extended."

"No. You can't do that," Erin argued. "You must spend the money on yourself. You deserve to spoil yourself."

I didn't want to play the guilt card, but I had to. I said, "Erin, I'll never stop feeling guilty over what happened to Robbie. But if you agreed to my plans, I know my guilt will be lessened. Don't you want me to feel better?"

Peggy joined in, "Yes, Erin, don't you want your sister to feel better? Stop being so selfish and let her help you."

Erin said, "You devious pair. You've got this all worked out, haven't you? May I ask what your plans are for my café once you've extended it?"

"First of all, I'm going to employ staff. Lots of staff. Erin, you can do the baking. No one else makes cakes like you do. But you won't be running around after customers. And you won't be on your feet all day. You can do your baking in the morning, and then that's it. You'll rest. You can stay at the café and talk to people, but no more being on your feet all day."

Robbie said, "I like the sound of that. Karis, you look as if you've got other plans for the café. Tell us."

"I thought we could run classes there. Perhaps during the day or after the café had closed. We'd have to get proper licences and insurance, but we can work those details out later."

"What sort of classes?" Erin asked.

Peggy said, "Anything and everything. We could start with craft classes. I know a lot about things like that. I don't like to blow my own trumpet, but I am good with my hands. I would love to teach others about crafts and things like that. I know the best places to get the cheapest materials. Erin, you could run some bakery classes too. I know I'd love that."

Erin gave her a slow nod. "Yes, I could do that."

I went on, "With the extended premises, we could cater to more people. You could have a quiet area with bookshelves so that people can read in peace. That area could be used for a book club too. And there could be a section for parents and toddlers. We could give the children a soft play area and the parents, or whoever is looking after the children, could have a cup of tea, a sit-down and a natter."

Erin nodded again. "I do like the sound of that. What else have you got up your sleeves?"

I reached into my handbag and produced a folder. I handed it to her. "As well as activities and clubs in the café, I thought Peggy and I could take our craft classes to those people who are housebound. We could take them some of your cake too. Free, of course."

"It would mean a lot to them," Peggy said. She paused for a few moments. "Loneliness is a terrible thing. People suffer in silence. If there's something we can do to help them, then we should."

Erin shared a look with Robbie. He gave her a gentle smile and a nod.

Erin declared, "Let's do this!"

I went over to her side and put my arm around her shoulder. "Thank you. There's one more thing. I want you to take it easy. You leave all the planning to me. I don't want you getting stressed. I mean it. You're carrying precious cargo."

"Okay, bossy boots. I can take it easy," Erin relented.

"Hallelujah!" Robbie cried out. "I've been telling her that for months."

"I'll put the kettle on," I said. "We've got lots to discuss."

I stood up and Peggy took my place on the sofa and began to give Erin more details about our plans.

I hadn't had any new visions about Erin yet. I hoped she'd take things easy now and give that baby the best chance of surviving that she could.

I had experienced other visions as I'd made my plans these last few days. They'd all involved Seb Parker. In each vision, he'd warned me to stay out of his murder investigation. The background changed in each vision. How many murder investigations was I going to get involved in? Would I be able to stop any of the murders?

I sighed as I filled the kettle. My psychic gift was a blessing and a curse, but if I could use it to help murder victims, then that's what I would do.

About the author

I live in a county called Yorkshire, England with my family. This area is known for its paranormal activity and haunted dwellings. I love all things supernatural and think there is more to this life than can be seen with our eyes.

I hope you enjoyed this story. If you did, I'd love it if you could post a small review. Reviews really help authors to sell more books. Thank you!

This story has been checked for errors by myself and my team. If you spot anything we've missed, you can let us know by emailing us at: april@aprilfernsby.com

You can visit my website at: www.aprilfernsby.com

Sign up to my newsletter and I'll let you know how to get a free copy of my new books as I publish them. You can sign up on my website. I'll also send you a Brimstone Witch short story as a thank you gift.

Many thanks to Paula for her proofreading work: https://paulaproofreader.wixsite.com/home

Warm wishes
April Fernsby

A DEADLY DELIVERY

Also by April Fernsby:

The Brimstone Witch Mysteries:

Book 1 - Murder Of A Werewolf

Book 2 - As Dead As A Vampire

Book 3 - The Centaur's Last Breath

Book 4 - The Sleeping Goblin

Book 5 - The Silent Banshee

Book 6 - The Murdered Mermaid

Book 7 - The End Of The Yeti

Book 8 - Death Of A Rainbow Nymph

Book 9 - The Witch Is Dead

Sign up to my newsletter and get a short story free as a thank you:
www.aprilfernsby.com

A Deadly Delivery

A Psychic Café Mystery

(Book 1)

By

April Fernsby

www.aprilfernsby.com

Printed in Great Britain
by Amazon